Chasi

By

Annabelle Jacobs

Copyright

Cover artist: Garrett Leigh
Editor: Sue Adams
Proof reader: Posy Roberts
Chasing Shadows © 2016 Annabelle Jacobs

ALL RIGHTS RESERVED:

This literary work may not be reproduced or transmitted in any form or by any means, including electronic or photographic reproduction, in whole or in part, without express written permission.
This is a work of fiction and any resemblance to persons, living or dead, or business establishments, events or locales is coincidental.
The Licensed Art Material is being used for illustrative purposes only.
All Rights Are Reserved. No part of this may be used or reproduced in any manner whatsoever without written permission, except in the case of brief quotations embodied in critical articles and reviews.

WARNING

This book contains material that maybe offensive to some and is intended for a mature, adult audience. It contains graphic language, graphic violence, explicit sexual content and adult situations.

Acknowledgements

Huge thanks to these lovely ladies: Jay Northcote, my super supportive alpha-reader and writing buddy; my editor Sue Adams, who makes me laugh with her comments and fixes my grammar, plot holes, and terrible misuse of commas; Posy Roberts who proof reads with an eagle eye, and my awesome pre-readers: Rachel Maybury, N.R. Walker, & Con Riley. You are all wonderful.

And an extra special thankyou to Rachel for answering my many, many questions about army men. I hope I did them justice.

Chapter One

The September sun shone brightly through the car windscreen, making Jamie squint. His sunglasses were somewhere on the passenger seat, and he grabbed blindly for them without taking his eyes off the road. After locating them, he slipped them on and relaxed back in his seat.

The Atlantic Highway was busy at this hour of the morning, but not as busy as it would be during the school holidays. Cornwall remained one of Jamie's favourite places; his family had come every year for as long as he could remember. His mum and dad made the trip every June to visit relatives in Padstow. Jamie and Michael tried to get down to Cornwall whenever they could, but it had been almost two years since Jamie had been back. He'd missed the rugged beauty and the smell of the sea.

He yawned widely, the lack of sleep starting to catch up with him. Leaving Nottingham at three o'clock that morning wasn't one of his better ideas, but he'd wanted to get an early start. Well, that wasn't strictly true. He hadn't been able to sleep and figured he might as well get up and go. Ever since Michael had stopped answering his phone or returning any of the numerous text messages and emails Jamie sent him, sleep had been hard to come by.

His brother wasn't known for his quick responses, especially when he got lost in his painting, but he never went more than a couple of days before getting in touch. It had been nine days since anyone had been in contact with him. Nine fucking days.

The ringing of his phone startled Jamie out of his thoughts. He slid his thumb across the screen to answer and put it on speaker. "Hello?"

"Jamie, sweetheart." His mother's slightly frustrated voice made him wince. Shit, he knew he'd forgotten to do something before he left. "Are you driving? I thought you were going to text me when you set off? You promised me you would."

Jamie sighed and ran a hand through his hair. "Yeah, sorry, Mum. I set off at three this morning—couldn't sleep. I forgot all about texting you." He heard muffled voices on the other end of the line, and then his dad came on.

"It's all right, Jamie, your mother just worries. We both do, since…." He let out a long breath, and it sounded like he closed a door. "Well, you know."

Jamie did know. They'd already lost one son, according to the police's theory. They didn't want to lose another. "It's okay, Dad. I should have texted. Sorry."

"So, where are you now, son?"

Jamie glanced up as he passed a road sign. "On the A39, about five miles past Bude."

"About forty minutes away, then?"

"Yeah, sounds about right."

Michael had been staying in a cottage near Polzeath. He'd rented it for a month, from August 28 to September 30. As it was still booked for another two weeks, Jamie had arranged to stop there, at least for the first few days anyway. The local police had given him the go-ahead. They'd already searched the cottage for anything to indicate where Michael might have gone, and the owners had emailed Jamie the code for the key box. Some might think it creepy to stay in the cottage after his brother had gone missing, presumed dead by the police and the coastguard, but Jamie didn't believe Michael was dead. Regardless of their efforts to be realistic about the situation, he was sure his parents didn't either.

They talked a little longer about what Jamie planned to do when he got there, and he promised to keep his mum and dad informed. They would have joined him, but his mum was recovering from hip surgery. His dad had been the one to come down to Cornwall when Michael had first gone missing, and Jamie had stayed in Nottingham with his mum. After two days of fruitless searching, his dad had returned to be with Jamie's mum, who wasn't coping too well, understandably, and there was only so much comfort Jamie could give her. His parents needed each other's support.

His dad hadn't gone to the cottage, his time taken up with the police and the coastguard. Jamie thought that was a blessing in disguise; the stress of being down here and seeing Michael's things wouldn't have done his dad any good.

"How're you both holding up?" Jamie kept an eye on the road signs. The last thing he wanted to do was miss the turn-off.

His dad sighed before answering. "We're hanging in there. Your mother's still not sleeping, but I can't say as I'm any better."

"Yeah," Jamie replied. "Me neither."

The last week had aged his parents. Hell, it had aged all of them. Michael's belongings were found abandoned on a secluded beach. A local fisherman spotted them and thought it strange when they were still there at nightfall. He informed the police, and the police had contacted Jamie as he and Michael lived together. At the beginning there'd been disbelief, then hope as the coastguard launched a search and rescue. But as the days passed with no word and no body, Jamie found himself becoming numb to it all. Even now it didn't feel real.

He and Michael had been close all their lives, despite Jamie being four years older. They'd moved in together soon after Jamie finished his degree and got a job — Michael jumped at the chance to move out of their parent's house. Jamie still hoped this was all a fucking nightmare he would wake up from any minute. It had to be.

Although the police weren't out physically searching for Michael anymore, the case would remain open and they had listed him as missing. Jamie didn't believe for one second that Michael had drowned. Something else had happened on that beach, and he was desperate to find out what.

After saying goodbye to his dad and promising to keep in regular contact, Jamie turned the radio up loud and tried to get lost in the music. He wanted to discover the truth about his brother's disappearance, but he also knew there was a good chance he might not like what he found, or worse, he might never know the truth.

Tresthelway Cottage sat at the end of a gravel driveway about two hundred yards from the main road. According to Michael, it belonged to the people who owned the farm next door, and this was the first year they'd rented it out.

Jamie climbed out of his car and paused to take in the peeling paint on the windows and the weeds littering the pathway to the door. The place had definitely seen better days, and from the look of the outside, the owners hadn't done much to smarten it up for tenants. No wonder it had been so cheap to rent.

The cottage was wide, with a couple of run-down outbuildings on either side. Rolling hills surrounded the place to the left and right — probably land belonging to the nearby farm — and although they were nice to look at, Jamie knew that alone wouldn't have been enough to draw his brother's eye.

The gate to the left side of the building opened with a loud creaking groan when Jamie pushed against it. It led down the side of the cottage — which was bigger than he'd first thought — and he followed it round to a large overgrown garden at the back. The still-damp grass reached mid-calf as he walked through it, and it wet the bottoms of his jeans, but Jamie ignored it, already smiling at what lay beyond.

Now he saw what had drawn his brother here and why the crumbling facade hadn't put him off. Beyond the brambles and weeds of the garden was one of the most beautiful views Jamie had seen. He walked closer to the wooden fence to get a clearer look at it. No wonder Michael had been so excited when he'd phoned.

The land at the back of the cottage sloped down towards the rocky cliffs below. Grass and wild flowers hugged a well-worn trail to the edge of the cliff where an old wooden bench overlooked the Atlantic Ocean. The sea shimmered in the distance as the sun set on it, looking wild and glorious as it crashed onto the rocks and sent spray into the air. Cornish beauty at its rugged best.

Jamie could easily picture his brother sitting on that bench for hours as he worked to capture the sense of awe the scene inspired. Once Michael found something worth painting, he took his time, studied and painted it from all angles. With this view on his doorstep, why had he felt the need to go elsewhere?

Hopefully something inside would give Jamie a clue, although the police had already been through Michael's belongings and questioned the cottage owners. Nothing they'd found indicated foul play, and as Michael was an artist, they assumed he went to the beach that day to paint.

With one last look at the sea, Jamie sighed and turned back to the cottage. He couldn't put it off any longer.

The small grey lockbox looked new and shiny and out of place. The lock also appeared to be new, so maybe the owners had made some attempt at bringing the security up to date, although he doubted the wooden door would keep intruders out for long, secure lock or no. He punched in the code and retrieved the key, but as he slipped it into the lock, a noise from inside had him freezing on the spot.

Jamie's heart stopped, and for one glorious moment he thought Michael had come back, but he held off opening the door as reality came crashing in. If his brother had suddenly turned up after being missing for nine days, he would have let someone know — probably Jamie himself.

He waited, straining to hear something else while wondering if his ears were playing tricks. The cottage wasn't exactly on the main road, and he hadn't passed any cars parked on the track that led there. An eerie quiet settled around him, the soft rustle of the wind through the trees caught his attention for a second until he heard the noise from inside the cottage again. It sounded like someone coming down the stairs with heavy footsteps. Either they didn't know Jamie was there or they didn't care, as whoever it was made no effort to keep quiet.

Shit. *What the hell do I do now?*

Carefully Jamie slid the key out and began to back away from the door. He tried to convince himself it was probably someone who had every right to be there — maybe the police had come back for another look, or it might be the owner.

But there are no other cars, his mind helpfully supplied. *Shit. Shit-shit-shit.*

With a shaky hand, Jamie pulled his phone out of his pocket to call the police. No way was he chancing an encounter with a possible burglar — he'd written too many stories of break-ins turned violent to risk disturbing whoever was in there.

9-9—

The front door burst open and startled him into dropping his phone.

"Bollocks!" Without looking at whoever had appeared, he bent down to snatch his phone off the ground and turned to run back to his car.

"Hey!"

Jamie faltered but didn't stop. He was almost at his car and had his keys out ready when a large hand clamped down on his shoulder and scared the shit out of him.

"Wait."

Chapter Two

Felix grabbed the guy and spun him around. He glanced down at the phone in the guy's hand. "Can you wait a second before calling the police?"

The guy's eyebrows rose almost to his hairline as he glared at Felix in disbelief. His thumb moved towards the phone screen and Felix reached out and snatched his wrist, pulling him back against his body and twisting the guy's arm so the phone clattered to the ground.

"Get the fuck off me!"

The guy yelled and struggled, but Felix held him tight, pinning him against his chest and keeping his arms secure.

"If you calm down for five fucking seconds and let me explain, then maybe I will." Felix had no problem keeping him restrained, the guy's muscles flexed under his hands in an effort to escape but Felix had about two inches on him in height and at least twenty pounds in weight. The guy wasn't small, but Felix was a big bloke at six foot three inches tall and he still trained as much as he was able. It made him strong and powerful, and he could hold this position for a good while yet. "I'm not going to hurt you."

The guy huffed and pointedly struggled against Felix's hold.

Felix leaned closer and whispered next to his ear. "I know plenty of ways to kill a man, and also how to inflict pain without it being lethal. If I wanted to hurt you, you'd be begging for mercy about now."

It took about two seconds for the fight to go out of him as the guy obviously realised he had no choice but to listen. "Fine. Go ahead and explain to me why you were in there. I'm all fucking ears."

The guy had balls, Felix would give him that. For someone in his predicament he still had plenty of anger and sarcasm to fling Felix's way. He might have given up the physical struggle, but his voice held no trace of resignation. Felix liked him already.

"I was looking for something."

"No shit."

Felix could almost hear the eye-roll in that reply and grinned despite himself. He tightened his grip a little, enjoying the way the guy winced at the increase in pressure. "Michael Matthews, the man who rented that cottage, disappeared nine days ago. I was trying to find any clues as to how he died."

The guy wasn't moving much before, but now he was rigid in Felix's arms, every muscle frozen for a long stretched-out moment. When he spoke, his voice was barely more than a choked-off whisper. "My brother rented that cottage, and he's missing, not dead."

Shit. "You must be Jamie." Although it might be a mistake, Felix released his hold and stepped back.

Jamie whipped around, rubbing his biceps, and glared at him.

Felix wasn't known for his bedside manner, but he wasn't usually that tactless. He wanted to kick himself for not noticing the family resemblance straight away. The hair was different; Michael had been dark whereas Jamie was blond, but now Felix thought about it, they had the same bright blue eyes and full lips. Felix had only seen Michael a handful of times, but he wasn't someone easily forgotten.

Even with the furious expression he was sending Felix's way, neither was his brother.

"How the fuck do you know that? And how do you know my brother?"

Felix didn't comment on the use of present tense. If Jamie wanted to go on believing his brother was still alive, that was up to him. In Felix's experience, missing people rarely turned up alive and well after that length of time. They came back in a body bag or not at all. He eyed Jamie curiously, wondering how much he could get away with. Jamie might be Michael's brother, but Felix hadn't known Michael and he didn't know anything about Jamie either. No way was he going to trust him with the truth.

"Well?"

Jamie had his phone in his hand again, but Felix wasn't worried about him calling the police just yet. He looked far too curious for that. Obviously Felix wasn't the only one after information. "I thought he might be involved with something I'm looking into."

"What the hell does that mean? Are you with the police?"

Felix sighed. "No." Jamie had a stubborn set to his shoulders and a glint in his eye that Felix recognised. Jamie wasn't going to let this drop until he thought he had all the answers.

Jamie nodded towards the open front door of the cottage. "If you aren't the police, you know that's breaking and entering, right?" He waved his phone between them. "I could report this right now and have you arrested."

"You could, but you won't." Felix might be pushing his luck, but he'd met plenty of men like Jamie—too curious for their own good.

"Oh, and why's that?"

"You think I have information on your brother's disappearance." *And with good reason.* Jamie was desperate to find out what Felix knew. No way would he risk that by having him arrested, heedless of the danger to himself. And Felix was dangerous; he hadn't been lying earlier. He could kill Jamie with his bare hands and not even break a sweat.

Not that he would... *Christ.* He wasn't some mindless killer, but Jamie didn't know that. People never ceased to amaze him with how careless they were when it came to their safety.

Jamie glanced down at his phone again as if considering his options, then shrugged and slid it into his back pocket. He met Felix's gaze, then let his own slide down over Felix's chest. "I believe you when you say you could kill me with your bare hands." He cocked his head to the side, considering. A slow smile spread across his face, and too late Felix realised he was stood with his feet shoulder width apart and his hands clasped loosely behind his back. "At ease, soldier?"

Felix glared at him and shifted position. "Ex-soldier. Still doesn't mean I won't hurt you."

For some reason that made Jamie visibly relax. The tense set to his shoulders was no longer there, as if the fact Felix had served his country meant he wasn't a threat. Felix shook his head. *Jesus.* He hated the way people were too trusting. That kind of mindset could get someone killed. *It has got someone killed*, his mind happily supplied. That was why he was here, after all.

"Look—" Jamie yawned and scrubbed at his face. "—I've had a bloody long drive and I'm knackered." He gestured between the two of them. "I wasn't expecting this when I got here, and I'm not exactly prepared to deal with it. But yes, you're right. I want to know everything you know, and it's pretty obvious I'm not calling the police. They're not interested in finding Michael. As far as they're concerned, he went for a swim and drowned. So any light you can shed on his disappearance, I want to hear about." He walked past Felix and into the cottage, pausing just over the threshold. "Coming?"

Felix shrugged and followed. What could it hurt?

Jamie led the way into the kitchen and headed straight for the kettle. "The milk'll be off, but I can make a black coffee?" He held up the tin of expensive barista-style coffee and shook it.

Felix grimaced but nodded. "Yeah, thanks." He rarely drank his coffee black, but Jamie wasn't the only one who was knackered. Felix had been up with the sun that morning, and he could do with the caffeine.

Jamie busied himself searching for mugs and a spoon while Felix leaned against the counter and watched. "So...." Jamie glanced over his shoulder before reaching up to the top shelf of the cupboard. Felix admired the breadth of his shoulders and the way they tapered down into slim hips. "You seem to know who I am. I think it's only fair I know your name."

Felix debated lying. He had no reason to trust Jamie Matthews, but for some reason he found the truth spilling out anyway. "Felix Bergstrom. My grandad was Swedish," he added when Jamie turned to look at him.

Jamie nodded. He finished making the coffees and handed a mug to Felix.

"Thanks."

"So, are you ex-Army, Marine, Navy?"

"Does it matter?" Felix set his mug down and crossed his arms. His departure from the Army had been the right course of action for him, he still believed that, but he missed his old life — the camaraderie, the sense of order that came with being a soldier — and it wasn't something he liked to talk about. Especially with a complete stranger.

Jamie sighed and took a sip of his drink, wincing when it burnt his tongue. "Shit," he hissed and sucked in a breath. He grabbed a glass from the cupboard and quickly downed some water before continuing. "Why are you interested in my brother? What possible connection could an artist from Nottingham have to you?"

"He was—" Felix stopped at the pained expression on Jamie's face. He had no doubt in his mind that Michael was dead, but he'd also been in Jamie's position. The people he'd lost weren't his brothers by blood, but they'd been the closest thing. Jamie had to come to terms with it in his own time, and Felix wouldn't try to force him to accept the truth. There was no body, after all, so maybe Felix was wrong, and if Jamie wanted to cling on to that hope, then Felix had no right to tell him otherwise. "The beach he's been going to for his painting, do you know why he chose that particular one?" Jamie frowned, so Felix elaborated. "It's not well known to anyone other than local residents, and the tides are so strong off that beach that even locals tend to give it a wide berth."

"I guess he liked the look of it. Michael loves to paint the sea, loves the raw power of nature in all its terrifying glory. His words, not mine." Felix hummed, not convinced. "How do you know this, anyway? Were you following him?"

"No." And that wasn't a lie. Michael had been in the same place at the same time almost every day, which Felix had started to think was more than coincidence. But Michael hadn't been his primary concern. He ignored Jamie's pointed look, choosing not to elaborate. "Out of all the beaches around here, why that one? It's not the most picturesque, and it's definitely a pain in the arse to actually get down to the sand, let alone carry all his art supplies with him. There are much easier seascapes to paint."

To Felix's surprise, Jamie threw his head back and laughed; the sound echoed around the quiet of the kitchen. "Oh my God, you've clearly never met any artists, have you? Well, none like Michael, anyway. If he saw something he was desperate to paint, he wouldn't give a shit how difficult it was to get to." He sobered up quickly, the smile falling from his lips. "Was that the same beach he disappeared from?"

Felix nodded. "Yeah."

"The police didn't mention that to me. They never said he'd been going there a lot, which makes their theory even more tenuous."

"How so?" Felix knew bits that he'd read in the local paper and from when the police questioned him: Michael Matthews, aged twenty-five; his clothes and personal effects were discovered on Saturday September 5 by a local fisherman. Felix had passed Michael's car at the side of the road that day. If he'd gone down to the beach too, then maybe he could have saved him, or at least seen what happened to him. Instead he'd driven farther along the road to watch the house on the hill.

"Michael loved to paint the sea, loved the way the waves crashed against the shoreline regardless of what lay in their path, but he would never have dipped so much as a toe in it, despite what the police think."

"How can you be so sure? The day he went missing was hot. It's not a stretch to think he might have fancied a cool—"

"He couldn't swim." Jamie cut in, his voice soft and fond. "We came to Cornwall every year and visited the most beautiful beaches, but Michael was frightened of the water. He was in awe of the natural beauty and spent hours looking out over the sea in rapt fascination, but not once did he want to swim in it. So the theory that he willingly walked into the water and went for a swim is ludicrous."

Felix's mind raced with that new and stunning piece of information. "Did you tell the police that?"

"Of course, but it only fuelled their suspicions. They said he probably intended to wade out only far enough to cool down but got swept away by the current and couldn't get back to shore." He stopped then, his gaze boring into Felix. "Nice deflection. I'm impressed."

For a second there, Felix thought he'd successfully steered Jamie away from asking about his connection to Michael. Apparently not. The silence stretched between them. Jamie was obviously waiting for Felix to tell him more, and Felix had no intention of doing so.

Finally, Jamie huffed and picked up his mug to take a drink. He set it down hard enough that a little spilled over the rim, and then he glared at it as though it were the mug's fault. "Are you just going to stand there and not say anything?" Felix shrugged. "You were inside my brother's cottage. I could still call the police about that. How did you get in, anyway?"

"Key." Felix fished the back door key out of his pocket and held it up for Jamie to see. "It was under a plant pot."

Jamie rolled his eyes. "Only Michael." As if he couldn't ignore it any longer, he reached for a cloth and wiped up the spilled coffee. "Why are you here? What exactly are you looking for?"

"That's none of your business."

Anything to connect Michael's death to Karl Weston, that was what Felix had hoped to find. Some scrap of evidence that would implicate Weston in at least one of the deaths he was responsible for. Indirectly, of course. A man like that would never get his own hands dirty. Weston's house on the hill overlooked Trelwick Beach. Felix didn't know if there was direct access to it, but it was too much of a coincidence as far as he was concerned. Michael must have discovered something that put his life in danger.

Jamie was in front of him in a flash, and Felix was grudgingly impressed he could move that quickly. "None of my business? For fuck's sake, my brother is missing and I find you here going through his things. You know something about his disappearance, and you can't stand there and tell me it's none of my fucking business."

Felix stood up straight and adjusted his jacket while Jamie continued to glare at him. "I don't know what happened to your brother or why. That's the truth."

"I don't believe you."

Felix's patience was running thin. He understood Jamie's frustration, but the last thing he needed was Jamie poking his nose where it didn't belong. "I don't give a fuck what you believe." He pushed Jamie back, hard enough to make him stumble, and headed outside.

"You will when I have you arrested for burglary!" Jamie shouted as Felix walked out through the open door.

Felix turned around and walked backwards, holding out his empty hands in front of him. "I didn't take anything and I had a key, so good luck with that." He smirked at Jamie's muttered curses and pulled the front door shut behind him.

The walk back to his car took him downhill through the trees as the dirt road dropped down to the stream at the bottom of the dip. He sloshed through the shallow water and then up the other side as an uneasy feeling settled in his stomach. If Jamie had any sense, he'd pack up his brother's belongings and head home.

But even from that short encounter, Felix knew Jamie wouldn't do that—he wanted answers. In his position, Felix would do exactly the same thing, *was* doing the same thing. As long as Jamie stayed out of Felix's way, they wouldn't have a problem.

Even as Felix thought that, he knew he hadn't seen the last of Jamie. And as much as he wished otherwise, a small a part of him looked forward to it.

Chapter Three

"What an arsehole!" Jamie yelled into the silence of the kitchen, refusing to look out the window and watch Felix walk away.

Who the fuck did he think he was? Poking around as if he owned the place and then refusing to tell Jamie what it was he'd hoped to find. Michael was Jamie's brother, and Jamie had every right to know.

He slapped his hand against the counter in frustration and seriously thought about reporting Felix to the local police. Jamie's phone was in his hand without him consciously taking it out, and he glanced down at it, his fingers hovering over the screen.

Would the police be interested in the break-in? Jamie thought about Felix's parting words. There was no sign of forced entry and nothing had been taken. It would be his word against Felix's, but as it was the home of a missing person, maybe they'd want to look into it. He should make the call, he knew he should, but a nagging feeling in his gut stopped him.

Felix knew something, that was obvious, and Jamie wanted to know what that something was. If he reported the guy to the police, the likelihood of him ever finding out would be zero. He slipped his phone back in his pocket, sighing heavily, and then jumped as it vibrated with a text message.

When he saw who it was from, he cursed softly under his breath and quickly dialled their number.

His mum answered on the first ring. "Jamie? Is everything okay? Your father said you should be there by now, and I—" The shaky breath she let out made his chest tight. His mum was happy and easy-going, but this whole nightmare had pulled the rug out from under her. "God, I'm sorry. You've probably only just got there, and the last thing you need is me pestering—"

"Mum, stop. It's fine." He walked through the kitchen with the phone pressed tight to his ear and stopped in front of the picture windows in the living room. The garden sloped away enough to give a view of the sea, and Jamie stared out at it as he spoke. "You're not pestering me. I should have called as soon as I got here. Sorry for worrying you."

She sounded better this time when she said, "I think we need to accept that everything worries me at the minute. So let's ignore that for now and pretend I'm not petrified every time you go anywhere."

Jamie smiled sadly. "Okay." The sun shone out between the clouds, bathing the garden in golden warmth, but Jamie struggled to appreciate the rugged beauty with his heart so full of loss. "What are your plans for the next few days? Are you going to be okay staying there?"

As far as his parents were concerned, he was down here to tie up any loose ends and collect Michael's things. The police still had his belongings from the beach, so Jamie would have to stop by the station at some point, but he'd planned on doing that tomorrow. Michael's car had been a rental; the police and the rental company should sort that out. Jamie could check with his dad. "Yeah, I'll be fine."

He glanced around the room, seeing a couple of pencils discarded over by the fireplace, an empty cup on the table, and Michael's grey hoodie slung over the back of the sofa. All signs that Michael had stayed there. Would Jamie be all right amongst so many reminders of what he'd lost? Uncertainty crept in and he clutched his phone tighter. "I'm going to go out and get a few basic supplies in a bit, maybe go for a walk to clear my head after the drive. I'll probably leave it until tomorrow to start packing up Michael's things."

"I know we've been through this, but I don't understand why you don't pack up his things today and come home. There's nothing for you there. Michael's gone." Her breath hitched and Jamie's eyes filled with tears.

"Mum...." He wiped at the tears as they spilled over. "I need to be here for a while. I can't explain why. Maybe to get some closure or something, I don't know, but I just need to. Okay?"

She took her time before answering, and when she did the resignation in her voice sent guilt sweeping through him. "Okay, sweetheart. Do whatever you need to."

He did need closure; he hadn't lied. But not the sort of closure she imagined. He wanted to find out the truth because not for one second did he think his brother had walked into the sea of his own accord and drowned. "Thanks, Mum, I'll call you tonight."

"Okay. Love you."

"I love you too. Tell Dad for me, will you?"

That was new as well. Two weeks ago his conversations with his parents ended with either a quick "bye" or "call you later." Now they ended every phone call with their love because, as they'd all learned in the hardest of ways, you never knew when it might be your last.

"Christ." Jamie slumped down into the overstuffed armchair and closed his eyes. With the drive, the run-in with Felix, and talking to his mother, Jamie was exhausted. Not only physically but mentally too. The past week and a half had passed in a blur of phone calls and heartbreak, and the crushing realisation that they might never see Michael again.

Jamie clung fiercely to the belief that his brother was alive, but as each day passed with no word, that fragile hope became harder to maintain. On the surface, his parents had accepted that Michael was dead. His dad had been there when the coastguard came back empty-handed, so maybe experiencing it first-hand had helped him. Maybe they were the realists in the situation and Jamie was fooling himself. But he and Michael were so close, had always been that way since they were kids. Surely he would know if his brother died? Wouldn't he feel something deep inside that told him Michael was gone?

He sat in the chair and let the silence wash over him. If Michael hadn't gone into the sea willingly, then either someone forced him in or took him from the beach and made it look like a drowning. Both scenarios sounded far-fetched when he thought about them, but what other explanation could there be?

God, his head ached with all the information running through it. He'd trained as a journalist and worked at the local paper for five years before going freelance, so he knew how to search for information. But this was different. Jamie had never felt so out of his depth. Where the fuck did he start?

The closest village to the cottage was about two miles away. Jamie wasn't in the mood to walk, so he unloaded his bag from the back seat of his car and drove there. Parking was easy; he found a spot outside the Spar shop.

Jamie grabbed a basket and did a mental checklist of what he needed: bread, milk, beer, bacon, and a couple of ready meals should do him for now. He'd have to go to the Tesco at Wadebridge if he planned on staying longer. The shop was empty, and the bored-looking cashier smiled up at him as he approached the till.

"Find everything you needed?"

The guy — Charlie, according to his name tag — was young. About eighteen or nineteen if Jamie had to guess, and he blushed when Jamie smiled back at him.

"Yeah, thanks." He watched as Charlie scanned the items.

"Do you need a bag?"

"Yeah, please."

"That'll be five pence, then." Charlie pointed to the sign above his head. "New rules." He shrugged apologetically as if it was his fault they now charged for carrier bags.

"That's fine." Jamie smiled again, trying to put Charlie at ease, but Charlie fumbled the milk carton and almost dropped it.

"Sorry," Charlie muttered under his breath, his face glowing with embarrassment.

Jamie took pity on him; he'd been that age once and knew all about being awkward in front of guys. "Hey, I don't suppose you could give me directions to Trelwick Beach, could you?"

Charlie paused, curiosity winning out over his mortification. "Yeah, I can, but why do you want to go there?"

"I've heard it's pretty and I fancied a walk."

"Well, it's okay, I guess." He paused to put the last of Jamie's shopping in the bag, then leaned closer over the counter. "But you might be better off going somewhere else. Someone died there a week last Saturday. It was on the local news and everything."

Jamie swallowed down the sudden lump in his throat. "Yeah, I heard."

Encouraged by Jamie's words, Charlie carried on, oblivious. "Apparently he came in here a couple of times. Sarah said she served him, but I don't remember. They're saying he drowned, but no one saw anything and they haven't found a body yet, so who knows?" He sounded almost gleeful, as if this was the most exciting thing that had ever happened, and Jamie had to bite his tongue to stop something harsh from coming out.

Charlie had no idea who Jamie was. As far as Charlie was concerned, he was sharing local gossip with a passing tourist, and it probably was the most excitement that this place had seen. It wasn't personal.

With great difficulty, Jamie ignored the heavy weight in the pit of his stomach and handed Charlie enough cash to pay for his shopping. "I also heard

Trelwick Beach is pretty hard to get to. It can't get many visitors, then?"

"Nah. A few of the secondary school kids go there sometimes. Sort of like a dare as most of them aren't allowed." Jamie smirked despite himself at the way Charlie referred to them as kids. He couldn't be more than a year or two older than some of them. "Some of the locals fish there too when no one's staying at the house."

Jamie looked up as Charlie handed him his change. "What house?"

"The one that overlooks the beach. Well, it doesn't exactly overlook it, but there's a path down to the beach from the garden. If you stand on the sand and look back up the hill, there's this big house on the left-hand side."

The shop was still empty, so Jamie leaned on the counter, seeing no reason to rush off when Charlie was so forthcoming with information. "Do you know who lives there?"

Charlie rolled his eyes as if that was the stupidest question ever. "Everyone knows everyone else's business around here. It used to belong to Mr. and Mrs. Cleary, but then she died of cancer. Their son, Adam, was in my class at school."

Jamie had the urge to hurry him along. The shop wouldn't remain empty, but Charlie was in full flow and Jamie daren't interrupt in case he stopped talking.

"Anyway" — Charlie waved a hand as though none of that was important — "they moved up north somewhere soon after. I think it was rented out for a while, but I'm not sure. Then, a couple of years ago, some bloke from London bought it."

"How come you know so much?" In Jamie's experience, teenagers didn't usually care about that sort of stuff. Maybe Charlie was just winding Jamie up, messing with the tourist.

Charlie glanced out of the window, then back at Jamie. "It's a small town, and when something like that happens, everyone talks about it. People were well pissed off with some stranger swooping in and snapping it up, especially when it turned out he'd only be in it the odd weekend every month. I mean, since then they've started building new houses on the outskirts of town, but it's not like there's a lot of housing to choose from around here. My mum ranted on about it for weeks."

Under other circumstances, Jamie would probably have taken the time to discuss this further. A few of his relatives in Padstow felt the same way. But today he was only interested in one thing. "Do you know the name of the bloke who bought it?"

Charlie grinned. "Yep. Karl Weston. He's been in here a few times. Seems all right. Bit flashy. That's probably why the olds don't like him much."

The door to the shop opened and a group of young girls wandered in. Charlie immediately stood up straighter, and Jamie took it as his cue to leave. The girls were all in school uniform, so it must be lunchtime. "Thanks."

He nodded at Charlie, but Charlie's attention had already drifted and he waved absently as Jamie turned to leave. Jamie laughed and shook his head. *Teenagers.*

By the time he got back to the cottage, he was hungry. The clock on the cooker read 12:35, so Jamie decided to have a quick lunch and head down to the beach afterwards. He wondered whether anyone was in the house, and had anyone been there when Michael went missing? Which reminded him.... He pulled his laptop out of its case and set it up on the counter next to him while he fixed himself a sandwich.

After wiping a stray bit of butter off the keys, Jamie typed "Karl Weston" into the search bar and waited to see what came back. He expected a few results. Karl Weston didn't sound like a common name, but probably not that rare either. Unfortunately there were far more than he thought, so he added "Trelwick Beach" to the search. Lo and behold a couple of results popped up. The first was a link to the local paper, and it looked the more interesting of the two so Jamie clicked on it.

"London Entrepreneur Buys Local Cornish Cottage as Weekend Holiday Home."

Clearly the news had been on the slow side that week if that made the headlines. The picture they'd used showed Weston leaving the local Spar, funnily enough. The angle wasn't brilliant, only the side of his face visible, but enough to see his short brown hair and brown eyes. In the photo he wore a dark suit that fit him like a glove, and even though he looked like he kept in shape, he did nothing for Jamie. Something about Weston's demeanour put him off. Maybe it was just a bad photo.

Jamie skimmed through the brief article underneath it, disappointed to find it didn't give him much more information than what Charlie had already told him. Except that "flashy" translated to "self-made millionaire." Karl Weston owned a car dealership, a cleaning firm, and a few other business ventures, all in London. It gave a little bit of his background, about how he'd started out with nothing and now had everything, according to whomever wrote the piece. They made him sound like a pop star instead of a successful businessman.

Weston wouldn't be the first person to snap up an idyllic cottage by the sea, and he wouldn't be the last. There was no crime in that. Jamie sighed and closed his laptop. He took his sandwich through to the living room and sat down on the sofa. A few brochures lay scattered over the coffee table, probably left out for Michael by the owners. Some of them had maps on the back, and Jamie remembered he hadn't managed to get directions from Charlie, after all. He hoped the beach was on Google Maps or he'd be in trouble.

Thankfully Jamie managed to keep his 3G connection for most of the way, and after ten minutes he pulled into a wide lay-by off the side of the road. The beach didn't have its own car park, and according to the map, this was the closest place to park.

He got out of the car and took a second to look around. Michael had a good eye. Even from up here Jamie could appreciate why his brother had come to this particular spot. The sky was that deep blue that always made Jamie smile, as though there was no other response to such a beautiful colour. A few clouds were dotted here and there, but otherwise it was clear.

The sun shone down on the sea below. The shimmering water appeared turquoise and so inviting it made Jamie itch to get in it. His skin was already a little clammy from the September heat. If he didn't have first-hand knowledge of Michael's fear of water, Jamie would be inclined to believe the police's theory. It wasn't hard to imagine someone wanting to cool off and then getting themselves into trouble when the currents took them by surprise.

But Jamie did know better, and they were wrong.

He grabbed his sunglasses from the passenger seat and locked the car. The tiny path to the beach led straight from the lay-by, cutting through the field at the side of the road before starting the descent down the hill. It weaved back and forth across the face of the slope until it finally widened out into a large sand dune.

The white sand spilled over the side of his trainers, so Jamie stopped to take off his shoes and socks before going any farther. It felt good underfoot; his toes sinking into the soft sand reminded him why he loved the beaches in this part of the country.

A couple of minutes later, after scrambling over a barrier of large flatish rocks, Jamie stood on a small stretch of beach. It might not be very big, but it was breathtaking. High tide was a couple of hours away, but from the looks of it, the sea didn't come in much farther than it was now.

Jamie walked across the sand, turning around slowly as he went, taking in the view.

Dark cliffs rose on either side, as if the beach had been carved out of them. The sloping hillside behind was the only way to get to it unless you came by boat. He paused, scanning the grass for signs of another path. After a few seconds, he spotted it. The one he'd walked down was well trodden, years of use turning it into an easy trail. The one leading up to the house was barely there; tall grass grew on either side, and Jamie doubted it got much use at all.

He tracked it as best he could, his gaze following the winding path all the way up until he spotted the top of a modern-looking house on the left-hand side, just as Charlie described. Only the top of the house was visible from where Jamie stood: huge picture windows and a wrap-around balcony. The effect was stunning, and who wouldn't want to make the most of that view? Jamie had been half expecting to see a cottage much like the one he was staying in, only better kept. This house, with its modern designs and extensive use of glass, was out of place in the wild landscape surrounding it. It screamed money, which Karl Weston obviously had plenty of.

Although Jamie would love to get a look inside that house and talk to Weston, he couldn't imagine someone with that much money inviting him in for a chat. Especially when they found out who he was. The police must have already interviewed him about Michael, and no doubt solicitors were involved. Talking about the case was something he'd probably been advised against. Besides, Jamie wasn't about to go banging on a millionaire's front door without doing a little more digging first.

Jamie gave the house one last look — maybe the officers in charge of the case would talk to him about Weston?

He turned and let his gaze sweep over the length of the beach again. According to the police, Michael's things had been found on the rocks at the far right of the beach — his rucksack containing a towel, a water bottle, and a couple of uneaten sandwiches, and also his painting supplies. Jamie walked over to the cluster of large rocks and tried to picture his brother sat there, looking out to sea and frowning in concentration. The image was far too easy to conjure up, and Jamie inhaled sharply at the sudden pain it brought with it.

"Fuck, Michael. What the hell happened to you?"

He slumped down in the sand and rested his elbows on his knees. The waves lapped gently at the shore, seemingly innocent, making it hard to believe that danger lurked beneath the surface. Jamie was well aware how easily a person could be dragged out by the strong currents, especially a non-swimmer. Would he ever find out the truth? Or would Michael become another statistic? A large part of Jamie wondered if it wouldn't be better to have the coastguard find Michael's body, then at least the family would know. No matter how horrible that outcome would be, they would have closure.

He shook his head, angry at himself for even entertaining the idea. Michael was alive; Jamie felt it in his gut, and he was a firm believer in trusting his instincts. With one last look out at the sea, he stood and brushed sand from his jeans. The beach made him uneasy all of a sudden. The hairs stood up on the back of his neck and he had the distinct feeling of being watched.

The house drew his gaze as he turned back towards the path, but it was impossible to see anything from this distance. Was anyone watching him from up there? Had they been watching Michael? Another question for the police. Jamie stopped at the top of the sand dune to tug on his socks and trainers. The sand stuck to his skin, and he gave up trying to get it all off, grimacing as the remaining grains rubbed against his toes when he walked.

The path felt a lot steeper on the climb back up. Jamie was clearly out of shape, judging by the way his thighs ached. He glanced up to see how far he had to go, and promptly stumbled, almost losing his footing altogether.

A man stood at the top looking down at him. Their gazes locked for a couple of seconds, and then he was gone.

Jamie stayed rooted to the spot, his heart banging against his ribs. The man's features were hard to make out with the glare of the sun, but he reminded Jamie of Felix. Maybe that was because Felix was the only person Jamie had met so far, apart from Charlie, but the build and hair colour matched. And Felix knew about this beach. Coincidence? Jamie didn't think so.

The ache in his thighs forgotten, Jamie hurried up the rest of the way. He was sweaty and out of breath by the time he reached the top. A quick glance left and right revealed he was alone. If it had been Felix, he was long gone. Jamie rested his hands on his hips, taking a minute to get his breath back. The trip to the police station might have to be sooner than he planned.

Chapter Four

Felix cursed when he saw the black Honda Civic parked in the lay-by, and he reluctantly pulled in behind it. He should have known Jamie would come to the beach to investigate. Weston's house wasn't visible from this spot, but Felix knew the man was there. He'd arrived back yesterday, which was unusual in itself. Until the past couple of weeks, Weston had only stayed at weekends, and even then not more than two per month, according to local gossip.

Since Felix had been watching him, Weston had been at the house more than he'd been in London. It screamed guilt as far as Felix was concerned, at least over involvement with Michael Matthews's disappearance, but there was no evidence linking him to any of it as far as Felix could ascertain. The police weren't very forthcoming with information, even though Felix had grown up with a couple of them.

Jamie's car was empty, as Felix expected, and he walked over to the start of the path to see if he could see him. And there he was, way down in the sand dune—balancing on one leg as he put his trainers back on. Felix watched, smirking as Jamie almost toppled over while tying his laces.

Felix wasn't sure what to make of him; their first meeting hadn't exactly gone well. Under different circumstances, Felix might have flirted a little, tried his luck. Sex was always a welcome diversion, and Jamie was easy on the eye. But hitting on a guy who'd just lost his brother wasn't something he was prepared to do. Nor did he think it would be well received. Besides, he had other things to concentrate on, and in this instance he probably shouldn't get distracted.

Once he had his shoes on, Jamie started walking again, and Felix watched him slowly make his way up. Just before he turned to leave, Jamie glanced up and saw him.

"Shit." Felix had meant to slip away unobserved. He stepped back from the edge and jogged over to his car. Another run-in with Jamie wasn't what he wanted, and by the time Jamie got to the top, Felix would be out of sight. Maybe Jamie hadn't recognised him; they'd only met once. Felix never forgot a face, but hopefully Jamie was different.

The main road curved, and Felix followed it past the turn-off to Weston's house. A couple of minutes later, he turned off onto a dirt track and parked on the grass verge about twenty metres in. It led to the fields at the back of Weston's closest neighbour's property. That was over a mile away, a farmhouse situated at the far end of the land, and only tractors came down this road. Felix had only seen one since he'd started leaving his car there, and the guy driving had smiled and waved as he'd driven past.

He walked back towards Weston's property, the wide-open fields leading to trees before too long. He stopped inside the tree line. A bright green lawn surrounded the house, split onto two levels with a gentle slope separating the two. No gate or wall protected the property, as Felix had half expected there to be the first time he came here, but Weston had installed security cameras along the roof. No one could approach the house without being picked up by whomever was monitoring the camera feed. Assuming someone was.

Felix had been coming here on and off for the past three weeks and hadn't been disturbed, so either he was out of range of the cameras or Karl Weston didn't give a shit that he was being watched. From what Felix remembered, Weston was arrogant enough for the latter to be true.

Felix settled down on the ground with his back against the nearest tree and pulled out his binoculars.

Let's see what you're up to this afternoon, then.

The canopy of leaves above his head shielded Felix from the afternoon sun, and he wiggled back, getting comfortable. He didn't usually spend all day camped outside Karl Weston's house, but he wasted a good few hours each day hoping to see something that would prove he wasn't wasting his time. Of course, if Weston did have anything to hide—*like a dead body*—then he could easily dispose of it at night or early in the morning, or any of the hours when Felix wasn't watching him.

When he thought of it like that, all this effort was pointless; he wasn't going to catch Weston doing anything illegal. But Felix's gut told him to keep coming back, so that was what he did, with his camera tucked safely in his backpack. There must be a reason Weston came back to the house more frequently than he had before, and Felix was going to find out what it was even if it killed him. A thrill of excitement rushed through his veins at the thought, because it wasn't a figure of speech where Weston was concerned. He was dangerous.

It had been a long while since Felix had been in the firing line, but this time he didn't have an SA80 to protect himself if it came to a fight. He glanced down at his hands and flexed his fingers. They would have to do.

About an hour later, a black Mercedes pulled up in front of the house. Felix raised his binoculars and focused on the car as both the driver and passenger doors opened. He quickly swapped the binoculars for his camera, cursing himself for not being quicker. The zoom was powerful, bringing the faces of the car's occupants into sharp relief. Neither of them looked familiar, not that Felix expected them to be, but Weston had had a few visitors before. Not these two, though.

They didn't fit the look of the car. From its license plate the Mercedes was only a couple of years old, and it gleamed in the late-afternoon sunlight, shiny and sleek. The two men who got out of it were anything but. They reminded him of gangsters from one of the old films his mother watched sometimes, with their greasy hair and ill-fitting suits. Felix might have laughed if there wasn't a strong possibility that they both *were* criminals. Or at least trouble.

They glanced around before walking up to the front door of the house. Who behaved like that in the middle of the Cornish countryside? Felix snapped off a couple of photos when they glanced his way. He thought back to Jason, his best friend and the reason why Felix sat on the ground, hiding amongst the trees as he watched for anything linking Karl Weston to the disappearance of Michael Matthews.

The police had listened when Felix told them Weston was involved in Jason's death. They listened and believed him when he told them everything he knew. He got the feeling they knew all about the nasty side of the millionaire businessman, but there was no evidence to suggest Weston was involved. Weston played his part as the grieving friend, much to Felix's disgust. The police politely told Felix to drop it. Jason's death was the result of a burglary gone wrong, and Karl Weston was not under suspicion.

That had been seven months ago.

And here he was all over again, watching Karl Weston get away with murder.

Felix wanted to kill him with his bare hands.

Weston walked out to meet the new arrivals. He clasped their hands in firm handshakes, one after the other, as though they were old friends. Maybe that's all they were; maybe Felix was being paranoid and seeing what he wanted to see.

He watched them go inside, but less than thirty minutes later, the door opened again and loud angry voices drifted over the distance. Gone were the easy-going smiles and welcoming handshakes, replaced with shouts and hand gestures. Some of the words were clear enough for Felix to pick out.

"This is your fucking mess I'm sorting out." Weston jabbed his finger between the two men as he yelled. "So you'll do what I say."

The response was too quiet for Felix to catch, unfortunately, but it made Weston drop his hand and nod sharply. The conversation carried on for a couple more minutes, and then the men got back in their car and drove away, kicking up gravel as they sped off.

What could have happened in under half an hour to go from smiles to that? Felix wished he'd heard both sides of that conversation.

He got lost in thought, watching the dust settle on the driveway, and only when his gaze flicked back to the front of the house did he notice Weston was looking straight at him. Could Weston see him? The trees should provide enough cover that he would be hard to spot, but the way Weston's gaze didn't waver made Felix think Weston knew exactly where Felix was.

Weston brought his hand to his forehead in a jaunty salute, then turned on his heel and walked back inside. He knew Felix was watching him, and he didn't give a fuck.

A cold chill ran down Felix's spine. What the hell was he even doing? This wasn't an episode of *Magnum, P.I.* and he certainly wasn't Tom Selleck — he silently blamed his mum for him even knowing who that was. He was an ex-Army sergeant, and he should know better than to get involved with people like Weston. If the police couldn't touch Weston, then what could Felix possibly hope to achieve?

The urge to leave was suddenly an itch under his skin. An uneasy feeling settled in the pit of his stomach, and it didn't look like abating any time soon. Felix stood and brushed dirt and leaves from his jeans, grabbed his backpack, and started to walk back towards his car. The safety of his own house sounded very welcoming right about then. He needed to regroup and decide what exactly he thought he could get out of this before going any further.

Yes, he wanted justice for Jason, but his friend had made some bad decisions leading up to his death, ignoring Felix's warnings and offers of help. As much as he'd loved Jason like a brother, he wasn't about to throw his own life away too. His family hadn't suffered through all those years dreading every unexpected knock on the door, only to have Felix get himself hurt, or worse, by sticking his nose in where it so obviously didn't belong. He needed to be more careful.

He went back to Weston's place early the next morning, unwilling to give up yet. Weston's BMW X5 wasn't there, but the black Mercedes was.

Weston didn't show all morning, and by lunchtime Felix had had enough.

What am I even doing here, anyway?

He moved silently through the trees, wondering how much longer he could keep this up. The odds of discovering any useful information were slim at best. What he needed was to get inside and have a look around, but that wasn't an option.

Felix reached his car, slung his backpack on the passenger seat, and headed for home.

His house was a good-sized two-bedroomed, two-story cottage. It sat at the foot of his aunt and uncle's property, about 100 metres from their big five-bedroomed house. They'd had the cottage purpose built for guests. Felix's family was large, and his aunt and uncle, living where they did, had a lot of visitors. Felix was still surprised when he turned onto the drive, and saw another car already there. Especially *that* car.

Fuck.

Jamie got out of his Civic as Felix parked and turned off the engine. He debated starting it back up and driving off, but Jamie was already walking towards him looking murderous, and Felix was curious to hear what he had to say. It helped that Jamie had changed into a tight pair of skinny jeans that hugged his thighs and his arse.

"How did you find me?" Felix asked as Jamie came to a stop a couple of feet in front of him. "I'm not listed as living here."

"The local police were very helpful when I popped in earlier. It seems you're on first-name terms with most of them." He raised an eyebrow, and Felix inwardly groaned — one of the drawbacks of living in a small community.

"Yeah, I went to school with some of them." Felix rubbed at the back of his neck and wondered how much his friends on the force had told Jamie. All of it was common knowledge to local residents, but he wasn't in the mood to have this conversation. "What were you doing at the station? Decided to report me for burglary after all?" He laughed dryly. "I bet that was fruitful."

Jamie sighed and looked down at the ground; his shoulders slumped as the anger appeared to drain out of him. "No. I went to see if I could pick up Michael's belongings. The police still have the things that were found on the beach." He toed at the loose gravel on the driveway and kept his gaze fixed firmly on his feet.

Felix felt like such a dick. "Shit. I'm sorry, I didn't think."

Another heavy sigh disturbed their peaceful surroundings, and finally Jamie looked back up. The pain in his blue eyes tugged at Felix's heart, and he cursed himself for getting involved. What happened to Jamie's brother was awful, but Felix had no business wanting to make Jamie feel better. It wasn't his job to offer comfort, no matter how badly his instincts screamed at him to do just that. Even as the thought ran through his head, he was already shuffling closer to rest a hand on Jamie's shoulder and give it a squeeze.

They stared at each other, neither speaking until Felix dropped his hand and took a small step back. Felix spoke softly. "Did they give everything back to you?" Jamie looked as though anything above a whisper would make him flee to his car. "At the station?" Felix added when Jamie didn't answer.

"No." Jamie reached up and rubbed at his eyes, then yawned. Felix imagined the last couple of weeks had been full of sleepless nights for Jamie and his family. "The officers in charge of the case weren't available. Not sure why someone else couldn't hand them over, but what do I know." Felix silently agreed with him, but Jamie spoke again before he could voice his opinions. "They were very helpful in other ways, though."

Jamie's gaze narrowed and Felix immediately bristled, the hairs on the back of his neck standing to attention.

Felix had a fair idea of what those ways were. It was only a matter of time, after all. "Oh?"

"Yeah. They offered me any assistance I needed while I'm here, and suggested if I wanted to know anything about the area, I should ask the cottage owners' nephew. Apparently he's looking after things while they're on holiday." Jamie shook his head. "Imagine my surprise when they told me his name."

Felix grimaced. "Yeah, about that—"

"Why the fuck didn't you mention that yesterday?" Jamie's voice rose, tinged with anger. "You didn't find that key under the plant pot did you, because you already had a bloody key. What the hell?"

Shit. Felix had no intention of telling Jamie everything, but he needed to come up with something. His actions probably seemed suspect, and he didn't want Jamie running back to the police station and complaining about him. That kind of attention wasn't what he was after. "Look, I'm sorry I didn't mention it when we first met. To be fair, I was a little surprised to see you there." Jamie scoffed but didn't comment. "My aunt told me you were coming, but I thought you'd arrive mid-afternoon."

"I had trouble sleeping." Jamie sighed, and the defeated set to his shoulders broadcast his feelings. "Still do."

Felix noticed the dark shadows under Jamie's eyes. He looked up at the sky and bit his lip. He liked Jamie, despite having only just met him. Felix tended to rely on his first impressions of people. Reading people was something he'd become good at, and he usually turned out to be spot on in the long run. Even so, he still thought it would be better for everyone involved if Jamie collected up his brother's things and went back home. Felix doubted that suggestion would go down well, but he'd make it anyway.

He sighed. "Yes, my aunt and uncle own your cottage. They own a couple more down the coast too, and I'm looking after them while they're away. In hindsight it was wrong of me not to tell you. I'm sorry."

"Is that it?" Jamie looked incredulous. "That's all you've got to say? I arrived yesterday to find you inside, searching through my brother's things, and you then lied about why you were there. Did you lie about knowing Michael too?" He backed away a couple of steps, and his gaze darted to his car and back.

It took Felix a second longer to realise Jamie was scared. Jamie stood his ground, fists clenched at his sides as he tried to hide it, but Felix recognised the look in his eyes. "Hey." He took a step towards him, with his hands held out in front of him. Jamie flinched but didn't move. "I understand why you don't trust me, but I'm no threat to you, and I wasn't a threat to your brother either. I met him once when I first arrived to introduce myself and let him know to contact me if he had any problems, that's all. But I did see him going to that beach enough to make me wonder if he knew Weston, the guy who owns the house overlooking it, and he's bad news. That was why I was in the cottage."

Jamie continued to glare at him. Felix got the feeling that Jamie only half believed him; he didn't look totally convinced by the explanation. Not that Felix blamed him. He wouldn't trust him either if he were in Jamie's position.

"I think" — Felix turned back to his car and pushed the driver's door closed — "the best thing for you would be to gather Michael's belongings and go home." Jamie narrowed his eyes slightly, but he remained silent. "There's nothing you can do here, and the police will contact you if they find anything." Felix twirled his keys around his forefinger and crossed the gravel until he came to a stop in front of Jamie. "What do you think?"

"I think you want me out of the picture so you can continue looking for whatever it is you think this Weston's involved in." He shook his head and glanced down at his feet before looking back up. "You don't give a fuck about what's best for me. You know nothing about me, so don't pretend otherwise."

With that, he turned and marched back towards his car.

Well, shit.

Felix watched Jamie stalk back to his Honda. In all likelihood, Jamie was going nowhere. If anything, Felix had piqued his interest even more and he would poke his nose into everything now. Felix shrugged and let his gaze wander down Jamie's back to his arse.

Might as well appreciate the view.

After climbing inside, Jamie slammed the door; the car skidded on the gravel as he sped off.

Something told Felix Jamie was only going to complicate matters, but he'd be lying if he didn't admit he found the prospect exciting.

Chapter Five

"Wanker!" Jamie hit the steering wheel. *Who the hell does he think he is?* The fact that what Felix said was true pissed him off even more. His mum would agree with Felix 100 percent—Jamie should do what he came down here to do and then return home. Back to his life.

He couldn't do that. Not with all the questions surrounding Michael's disappearance. No way could he even start to pick his life back up until he had some answers, and instinct told him Felix was the key to getting them.

And wasn't that the icing on the fucking cake?

Jamie had all sorts of confused feelings about Felix.

Was he dangerous? Undoubtedly. As an ex-soldier, he could probably kill Jamie without breaking a sweat. Was Felix a danger to him? Jamie didn't get that feeling from him. He was definitely lying or withholding information, but apart from yesterday morning when he arrived at Michael's cottage, Jamie hadn't felt threatened by him. Well, maybe for a couple of seconds outside Felix's house too…. The vibe he got most, though, was that Felix thought Jamie was a pain in the arse—a complication. Especially with the way he'd told Jamie to go home.

Well, he could just fuck right off. Jamie would go home when he was ready, not when some muscled arsehole told him to. An image of Felix's broad shoulders slipped unbidden into his head, and he pushed it away with an irritated huff, seething silently all the way back to the cottage.

The anger drained away as soon as he pulled up in front of the house and turned off the engine. The shabby exterior gave the front of the cottage a quaint appearance, a homey, lived-in look that promised a warm and cosy interior. But with Michael's things strewn about the place as he'd left them, cosy and inviting it was not.

Jamie let his gaze travel over the well-worn front door, tapping his thumbs on the top of the steering wheel. As much as he'd like to ignore it, putting off sorting out his brother's things was pointless. The sooner he started, the sooner it would get done. With a heavy sigh, he climbed out of his car and headed inside.

The cottage had two double bedrooms. Jamie had only poked his head in the master one yesterday. The sight of the crumpled bed sheets and Michael's clothes left on the floor had reminded him so much of their flat in Nottingham that he'd shut the door quickly and hadn't been in since.

He ducked his head as he climbed the narrow stairs. The ceiling stood at least a foot above his head, but it felt as though he'd bang it any second. The carpet felt thick and soft under his socked feet. He paused on the top step, steeling himself.

The door to Michael's room was to the left, and it opened easily when Jamie turned the handle. An eerie creak filled the air as it swung wide and came to rest against the wall. Jamie took the couple of steps to get him over the threshold and then stopped.

It had been late evening when he'd glanced in before, with not enough daylight to see everything clearly, and he hadn't stayed long enough to turn on the light. Now the sun shone in through the open curtains, displaying everything with stark clarity. Jamie stood inside the doorway and forced himself to take it all in. Maybe he would get lucky and see something — anything to give a hint as to what had happened to his brother.

The bed was unmade; the heavy quilt and top sheet were pushed to the foot of the bed as though they'd been kicked there when Michael got up. Jamie frowned out of habit. It had always annoyed him that Michael never made his bed. A black suitcase sat on the floor under the window, and when Jamie walked over to it and lifted the lid, he found it was still half-full with clothes.

He shook his head and smiled despite himself. Michael really was a lazy fucker. He never put his clothes away, even at home, and Jamie was going to rib him about it mercilessly the next time he saw —

Shit. The realisation made his stomach swoop and his chest ache.

There wouldn't be a next time.

He stumbled over to the bed and sat down on the edge, his hands shaking as the fresh wave of hurt washed through him. It had been like that since they got the news. Jamie couldn't think about it all day, every day. Something would take his mind off Michael and he'd be okay for a while, and then without warning the little things would bring it crashing down and he would have to collect himself all over again.

He sat there waiting for the worst to pass, breathing steadily in and out; he looked around the rest of the room. Apart from the pile of clothes on the floor, it was surprisingly tidy. Maybe Michael only slept in there. With the scenery surrounding them, Jamie guessed he'd spent most of his waking hours down at the beach or in the back garden. Jamie stood and shook out his arms, relieved his hands no longer shook. The window opposite the bed had a big wooden bench seat underneath it, and when Jamie walked over to it, he saw why it was there. This bedroom faced the sea.

He smiled as he sat and looked out at the waves in the distance. Michael must have loved it there. When Jamie leaned back against the wall, he caught sight of something half covered by the bottom of the curtain. Leaning forward he snagged the corner of it and tugged it towards him.

Michael's sketchbook.

Jamie flipped open the first page and promptly let it fall closed again as he recognised the drawing. Michael had done it as a joke when Jamie fell asleep after Christmas lunch. It was incredibly unflattering, and Michael had taken great delight in showing everyone he could.

Maybe Jamie would look through it later. He set the book carefully to one side and got up to check the rest of the room. Despite the amount of clothes still in the suitcase, the drawers in the bedside cabinet were full of socks and boxer briefs, and the wardrobe shelves held a pair of jeans, some shorts, and a pile of T-shirts.

Jamie moved the case onto the bed and started to pack up Michael's clothes, letting his mind wander to anything else while he did it. The fact that his thoughts strayed to Felix didn't come as much of a surprise. Even in the shittiest of circumstances, there was no denying Jamie found him attractive—frustrating and intimidating too, but maybe that was part of the appeal. Not that Jamie had any intention of pursuing him. Felix might be hot, but he was also a liar, and Jamie didn't trust him at all.

Focusing on Felix did serve to take Jamie's mind off what he was doing, though, and before too long he'd packed up Michael's belongings and the suitcase was full. He made the bed without thinking about it, smoothing down the quilt and fluffing up the pillows. Placing the sketchpad carefully on top of the case, he left them both where they were and headed back downstairs.

Fresh sea air sounded very appealing all of a sudden, and Jamie walked through the living room towards the patio doors. A sharp rap on the front door stopped him in his tracks and his heart skipped a couple of beats.

Who the fuck could that be?

They knocked again and Jamie startled, shaking his head at his skittishness. Nothing sinister was going to happen; it was just someone at the door. God, he'd been watching too much TV lately. With a sigh, he walked back towards the front door, and pulled it open.

Felix stood on the other side, and Jamie didn't know why he was so shocked to see him there. It wasn't as though he knew a lot of people in Polzeath. Felix had what looked suspiciously like a cake tin in his hands and a resigned expression on his face.

Jamie glanced down at the tin and then back up at Felix. He raised one eyebrow. "Have you brought me cake?" Felix shifted from foot to foot; his body language screamed that he'd rather be anywhere than on Jamie's doorstep. Then why was he there? "Um...." Confused, Jamie was lost for words. Out of all the imagined scenarios, he'd not pictured this when he went to open the door.

Felix rolled his eyes. "My aunt phoned, and when I happened to mention you'd arrived, she was horrified that I hadn't welcomed you properly. Apparently she greets all her guests with homemade scones, clotted cream, and jam. No matter the circumstances."

Jamie's mouth watered and he turned his gaze on the cake tin again with renewed interest.

"They're not homemade," Felix added after a pause, "but it was the best I could do on short notice. And to be fair, the bakery in the village is pretty good, far better than anything I could manage."

"You bake?" Jamie's head snapped up.

"Yes, it has been known. I can cook too. Don't look so surprised." Felix thrust the tin towards Jamie, forcing him to take it. "So can I come in, or shall I leave these with you?" He pulled a rucksack off his shoulder and began to rummage inside it.

"No, come on in, sorry." Jamie finally remembered his manners and beckoned Felix inside. He had brought scones, after all. The least Jamie could do was make him a cup of tea. This unexpected turn of events had him off-kilter, and he was curious to see where it might lead.

He followed Felix into the kitchen and leaned against the counter, watching as Felix unloaded a carton of clotted cream and a jar of strawberry jam.

"This is homemade, though." Felix picked up the jam and waved it in Jamie's direction. "My aunt makes all her own jam and marmalade." He set it back on the counter.

Jamie was struck again by how surreal this was. Less than two hours ago, he'd have cheerfully strangled Felix, and the feeling was no doubt mutual, but here they were about to have scones and cream like civilised people.

"Shall we have some now?" Jamie rubbed his belly, realising with a pang that he'd missed lunch.

Felix's expression was a mix of surprise and confusion. "I brought them for you. Don't feel obligated to share them." He slung his rucksack back over his shoulder.

Jamie wanted to groan in frustration. If Felix hadn't wanted to share them, then why insist on coming inside?

Jamie grabbed the kettle and turned the tap on to fill it. "I'm sure there's far more in that tin than I could eat, so why don't you sit down and join me?" He turned his back on Felix while he set the kettle on its base and flicked it on, giving Felix time to decide what to do. Yes, Jamie might have ulterior motives besides being friendly, but he still had a ton of questions he wanted to ask Felix, and Felix must know that. If they were both interested in the same thing, wouldn't it be beneficial to share what they knew?

He turned and crossed his arms, regarding Felix expectantly. "Well?"

Felix met his gaze. His blue eyes bored into Jamie and made him want to stand up straight and uncross his arms. Felix nodded. "Okay, if you're sure."

"I am."

The kettle bubbled behind him as it came to the boil, and Jamie busied himself with making two mugs of tea, conscious all the while of Felix watching him. The feeling both unsettled him and sent a curl of heat up his spine.

All of a sudden, the kitchen felt too enclosed, the tension in the air was stifling, and Jamie wanted to shrug off the feeling before it threatened to overwhelm him. "Let's eat outside."

He waited for Felix to object, just to be difficult, but instead Felix opened the cupboard above him, grabbed two plates, some cutlery from the drawer beside him, and finally a tray from down the side of the fridge.

It irritated Jamie how well Felix knew his way around the kitchen, which was an irrational feeling since Felix had probably been here many times before. Still, for now this was Jamie's home, no matter how temporary, and he couldn't help it. With a frown he picked up the two mugs of tea and followed Felix and the tray of scones out onto the back patio.

Only half of the table was in direct sunlight, and Jamie immediately chose one of the shadier chairs. He hated eating in the sun. Felix did the same and then began to unload things from the tray.

An uncomfortable silence stretched between them. They weren't friends, or even acquaintances. Jamie didn't know what they were exactly. Yet here they sat having afternoon tea. Bizarre was the first word that sprang to mind.

"So." Jamie sat forward in his chair. He'd never been one to let a silence go on if he could help it. Felix glanced at him, opened the tin, and helped himself to a scone. "How do you know Karl Weston?"

If he hadn't been watching closely, Jamie would have missed the way Felix tensed before continuing to cut his scone. "I'm not stupid. You let slip earlier that you thought Michael might have known Weston. That's why you were in the cottage. Why would you care about that if you didn't have some connection to him?"

Jamie hadn't picked up on it at the time, too angry to concentrate on what Felix was saying. But it had sat in the back of his mind as he'd sorted through Michael's things upstairs. Why mention Karl Weston in relation to Michael? Why was Felix so interested in a connection?

He tapped his fingers on the wooden tabletop as Felix took his time spreading jam and then cream over one half of his scone. Finally he set his knife down and sat back in his chair.

"I knew him years ago when he was in the Army."

Well, that wasn't what Jamie had expected him to say. He leaned close, his curiosity piqued. "And?"

Felix sighed, playing with the edge of his plate as if debating how much to say. Jamie wanted to know everything, but he doubted he'd get the whole story. Still, anything would be better than what he knew at the minute.

Felix fixed Jamie with an undecipherable look. "He was in my regiment. We met after basic training: me, him, and Jason Stewart." He took a sip of his tea and set the mug back down heavily. "Weston left after his four years were up, and I never heard from him again."

Jamie waited for him to continue, but Felix picked up his scone and bit into it, effectively ending the conversation.

As far as stories went, that one was a bit anticlimactic. Jamie busied himself slathering cream on his own scone while thinking of what to ask to get Felix to continue. "What about the other guy, Jason? Does he still keep in touch with him?" Maybe whoever he was had a better insight into Weston.

Felix flinched as though Jamie had slapped him, and Jamie knew without Felix having to say the words. "Jason was killed last year."

Fuck.

"In combat?" Jamie asked softly, wondering whether or not he should let the whole subject drop. He saw it on the news all the time — soldiers killed in action — and was ashamed to say he didn't pay much attention to it. Guilt swept through him at the lost expression on Felix's face. He couldn't imagine living through it and losing people that way.

"No," Felix answered after a pause, his voice as soft as Jamie's had been. "Jason left the Army at the start of last year. He was attacked when his flat was burgled. Head injury and stab wounds. Police said it was the head injury that killed him."

Jamie sat in stunned silence, not expecting that answer and at a loss how to respond. "That's shit," he mumbled.

Felix let out a harsh laugh. "Yeah, it really is."

They lapsed into silence again. Jamie's appetite had disappeared, and he pushed his plate away. Felix had shared more than he'd expected. Regardless of Jamie's words to the contrary, Felix didn't owe him any explanation. Jamie just wanted one, and he felt compelled to offer up some of his own story to even the playing field. "Michael went missing sometime on Saturday, but the police can't be sure when. He texted me Friday night—a quick message to let me know he'd found a great place to paint and he'd call soon." Jamie paused to drink his tea, grimacing when it had cooled too much. "I replied with 'That's great, talk soon.' And nothing else. Those were the last words I sent to my brother. I know it makes no sense to regret it, because how was I supposed to know they'd be the last, but I can't help feeling like shit about it. I couldn't manage more than a four-word reply because I was in the middle of watching a fucking film."

He jumped when Felix put a hand on his shoulder, squeezing once with his strong fingers before letting go. This was the second time Felix had touched him, comforted him. The warmth lingered, making Jamie wish Felix had kept his hand there. He glanced up to see Felix watching him intently.

"Jason was my best friend. He called me two days before he died. We argued. I told him he was a fucking idiot and hung up."

Felix scrubbed a hand over his face, and Jamie had the sudden urge to pull him in for a hug.

Christ. He felt worse now than when he'd been packing Michael's things. For two virtual strangers, the conversation had been more personal than Jamie was comfortable with. He wasn't sure how that had happened, but it left him off balance. He eyed his scone again and bit into it for something to do, hardly tasting it.

"I should go." Felix stood abruptly and his chair scraped along the patio slabs. "Feel free to contact me if you have a problem with the cottage. Number's on the fridge."

With a nod he was gone, walking briskly around the side of the house.

Jamie sat there staring after him. What a weird fucking day. Instead of finding out what had happened to Michael, Jamie had more questions than he did before. He drew his phone out of his pocket and called his mum.

"Hey." He smiled into the phone as she picked up. "How are you and Dad?"

"Well, I'm not too bad, but your father's fussing is driving me up the wall!"

She muttered something under her breath that Jamie didn't quite catch, and then he heard his father's voice in the background. He relaxed at the familiar sound of fond bickering. It was good to hear them like that again; the last few days had been draining for everyone. "What did he say?"

His mum sighed. "He thinks I'm trying to do too much and that I'm rushing things."

"Are you?" His dad was probably spot on. Jamie could easily imagine his mum getting fed up with being so inactive. "You only had surgery five weeks ago, okay. You should still be taking it easy."

"Please, not you as well. Anyway, enough about me. When are you coming back home?" Her tone softened. "Have you packed Michael's things up at the cottage?" The sadness in her voice made Jamie's chest ache.

"Almost. I just need to get some stuff from the police station."

Her breath hitched, and Jamie cursed himself for bringing it up. "Oh, o-of course. And then?"

"Yeah, about that. I, um...." He deliberated what to say next. Talking to Felix had piqued his curiosity, and maybe it was the reporter in him, but he couldn't go home yet. There definitely seemed more to Michael's disappearance than the police were suggesting, and Jamie wanted to dig a little further. He might come up empty-handed, but if he left without even trying, he would feel like he'd let Michael down. His brother deserved more than two days of Jamie's time. "I think I'm gonna stay for a week. The cottage is all paid up and I've already booked the time off work, so—"

"Sweetheart, it can't be healthy staying there after... well, it just can't be. The police will let us know if they find anything, so please come home. There's nothing you can do down there now."

"Come on, Mum. I need to do this. We all know Michael didn't drown by accident."

"Jamie...."

"The police are wrong. I don't care how hot it was or how appealing the water looked, he would never have gone in that bloody sea. I'm not even convinced he's dead, and I don't think you and Dad are either. You just refuse to admit it."

Silence on the line told him he'd gone too far. *Shit.*

He ran a hand through his hair. The last thing he wanted to do was upset her, but they'd all tiptoed around the subject for too long and he needed to talk about it. "Look, I'm sorry, Mum, I shouldn't have said all that. But I need to do this."

The silence continued for so long Jamie thought she'd hung up, but then she sniffled and he closed his eyes, feeling like the shittiest son ever. "When we first got the call about Michael, both your father and I were adamant that they were wrong. We told them Michael hated the sea, and he would never willingly put more than a toe in it. And for the first day or so, we fully expected him to turn up with some excuse or other. But he didn't, and it's been ten days, Jamie. Ten days with absolutely no word from him." She took a shuddering breath, and Jamie clenched his phone tight as the pain gripped him. "As hard and as awful as it is, you have to accept that something happened to him on that beach. And yes, you're right, until they find a... until they find him, a small part of me will always hope that he's coming home, but for our own sanity, your father and I are trying to accept the possibility that Michael is gone."

Guilt weighed heavily on Jamie as he clutched the phone to his ear. Was he being selfish by wanting to stay? His mum and dad were clearly trying to come to terms with it, and he wasn't helping matters by voicing his doubts. He should have kept it all to himself; they'd gone through enough already. *Fuck it all.*

Another heavy sigh on the line reminded him his mother was waiting for him to reply.

"I'm sorry. I know how hard this past week has been on you and Dad, and I didn't mean to make it worse."

"I know you didn't, and I'm sorry for going off like that. We all have to deal with it in our own way. You do what you need to do and come home when you're ready. Okay, love?"

God, his mum was the best. "Okay. I'll keep in touch."

"You'd bloody well better." Her voice was still a little shaky, but Jamie heard the smile in it too. "Love you."

"Love you too." He ended the call and set his phone on the table.

The wind had picked up, and Jamie shivered as he stood and began to collect everything to put back on the tray. Now that he'd decided to stay, he needed a plan of action.

Chapter Six

Felix drove back to his house, wondering why he'd felt the need to tell Jamie about Jason. And Weston, come to think of it. He didn't owe Jamie an explanation, but the regret in Jamie's voice when he'd talked about his brother had struck a chord. Felix knew all too well how that felt and the words had come tumbling out. He'd spent weeks torturing himself over the last conversation he'd had with Jason, hating the thought that Jason had died thinking Felix didn't give a shit about him.

It had taken a very frank and honest talking-to from his other mates, Nick and Adam, to snap him out of it. They were still in the Army, had served over twelve years with him and Jason, and after the funeral they'd taken Felix to the pub and told him to snap the fuck out of it. The pair of them stayed with him until he accepted that one stupid argument didn't erase years of friendship. Jason hadn't died thinking Felix didn't care.

He'd wanted to share that sentiment with Jamie, but wasn't sure he'd succeeded. Felix had felt out of place sitting outside eating scones, for fuck's sake, and in the end he'd had to leave. If he didn't have such a soft spot for his aunt, he would never have taken the bloody things round to Jamie in the first place.

The turning to his house came up sooner than he was expecting, but instead of taking it, he carried straight on. He felt far too restless to go home yet, and without realising it, he ended up at the dirt track behind Weston's property again.

Might as well get out as he was there.

He grabbed his backpack out of the boot, and picked his way through the trees until he reached his usual spot. Weston's house looked as it always did: immaculate and cold. Weston's X5 now sat outside, with the black Mercedes nowhere to be seen. Felix leaned back against the nearest tree and wondered what had made Weston buy this place. It had to be coincidence that he'd bought a house where Felix grew up. Sure, they'd all talked about home when they were stationed together, but that had been years ago, and he and Weston hadn't spoken once since the day Weston left. Jason was the only one who'd kept in touch with Weston. Felix had never understood why. Weston had turned into a right wanker at the end, and everyone had been glad to see the back of him. Well, everyone apart from Jason, but then, he liked everyone.

Felix blew out a breath, welcoming the familiar ache that came when he thought about Jason. What a fucking waste.

Movement in front of the house caught his attention and he straightened, immediately alert. The side door swung open just as the Mercedes pulled up in front. Where had they been, then? The same two guys got out to meet Weston.

Whatever they'd argued about the day before seemed long forgotten. Weston smiled at them both and clapped them on the shoulder as he passed. He threw something small to them, which one of them caught, and then turned towards his double garage. Felix watched with interest as Weston went inside, and then moments later another BMW—a dark blue

M3 — reversed out and stopped behind the cars already parked there.

Flash bastard.

Weston stayed in his car until one of the other guys went back in the house and came out carrying a small suitcase. Felix shook his head as the man went around to the back of the car and put the case in the boot. What a lazy bastard. As soon as the boot slammed shut, Weston spun the car around, spitting gravel everywhere and almost knocking down the guy in the process.

Still a wanker, then.

The guy shouted something and gave Weston the finger as soon as he was out of sight. Felix grinned; clearly he wasn't the only one who thought so. Even Weston's own people hated him. All that aside, Felix wondered why Weston needed house-sitters while he was away. He didn't have any animals; well, not that Felix had seen.

It probably meant nothing, just Felix's overactive imagination getting the better of him. Years of being cautious and assuming the worst had made him suspicious of everything. It was a hard habit to break. Both guys finally went inside Weston's house and all was quiet again.

Felix yawned and rubbed his eyes. *What the fuck am I even doing here?*

He'd been watching Weston's place for almost two weeks now, and seen nothing. Probably because there was nothing *to* see. If the police couldn't get anything on him, then what hope did Felix have? None. He was wasting time on a man who couldn't give two fucks about him and probably laughed when he saw him out there. Christ, if Nick and Adam could see him, they'd take the piss and tell him what an arse he was being.

Jason was dead. Nothing Felix did would bring him back, and despite what he knew in his gut, Weston appeared squeaky clean.

Maybe it was time to call it a day and focus on his own life instead. He thought of Jamie and Michael, but dismissed it before he began to feel guilty again. That wasn't his problem. With one last look at the house, Felix grabbed his bag and slung it over his shoulder. He'd wasted enough time on Karl Weston. Hopefully karma would do its job and Weston would pay eventually.

Felix hummed to the radio as he drove back to his own cottage. Watching Weston had taken most, if not all, of his spare time recently, and if he didn't plan on doing that any longer, then there wasn't a lot else to do. All of his aunt's three rental properties were currently occupied, so he couldn't very well check on them, and he didn't know anyone well enough to socialise with. Felix had left this part of the country fourteen years ago, and any friendships he'd had back then had fallen by the wayside when he joined the Army.

He was going to be bored.

At times like this, he fucking missed Army life. His mind wandered back to the friends he'd left there. The last he'd heard from Nick, they were due back in the UK on September 14. It was a long shot, but….

As soon as Felix arrived home, he turned off the ignition and grabbed his phone. He wasn't a big fan of texting, so he fired off a short, succinct message to Nick and Adam asking them if they were back in the country yet, because he was bored. Not expecting a reply anytime soon, he pocketed his phone, got out of the car, and went inside.

Early the next morning, as Felix wrestled with the lawnmower—damn petrol mower always took a good few pulls to get going—his phone rang, startling him. After wiping his hands on his jeans, Felix answered the call on the fourth ring. "Hello?"

"Took you long enough to answer, you lazy bastard. Too busy sitting around on your arse?"

Adam sounded loud in his ear and Felix grinned. God, it was good to hear his voice. "Fuck off. I'll have you know I'm in the middle of landscaping my aunt and uncle's garden."

"Really?" Adam sounded a mix of sceptical and reluctantly impressed, and Felix tried to cover his laugh with a cough. "You are so full of shit."

Felix's grin got wider. "Yeah. Well, I was about to mow the lawn."

Adam laughed. "That sounds more like it. Look, I'm heading out in a few, but wanted to catch you before I left. Me and Nick are on leave this week. We'll be down tomorrow."

That was sooner than Felix had expected and his mood lifted immediately. "Bring a sleeping bag if you don't want to share with Nick. There's only one spare bed. See you tomorrow." They ended the call, and Felix leaned heavily on the mower, his smile still huge and not going away anytime soon.

This whole situation with Weston, and now Jamie, was starting to get to him. Felix knew better than to rake up the past. You couldn't change it, so why waste time worrying about it. When he'd found out about Weston's holiday home in the village where Felix grew up, he'd jumped at his aunt's offer of work. He'd thought he could kill two birds with one stone, but he should have left Weston well alone and just enjoyed the Cornish countryside while helping out family.

He had a contracting job lined up after this, as a project manager, but wasn't due to start until October 19. Felix vowed to make the most of the weeks left, and with that in mind, he tried to start the mower one more time. The sky was blue, with the sun burning off the last of the morning haze. A day working outside in the garden would pass the time nicely.

Usually at this time of day, he was camped out in the woods watching Weston's house. He ignored the feeling that he was missing something, rolled his shoulders, and shook it off. This was a much better use of his time. Finally the roar of the mower filled the air, and Felix lost himself in the steady work of cutting the grass.

Wednesday passed without anyone visiting or calling. Felix couldn't remember the last time he'd stayed at the cottage all day. He'd half expected Jamie to turn up and badger him for information again. When the day passed without so much as a phone call, Felix was more than a touch disappointed. Which was ridiculous. He didn't want to get involved with Jamie and his theories about his brother's disappearance. That was none of Felix's business.

He whistled as he walked down the stairs on Thursday morning. The night before had been hotter than normal, and Felix had slept in only his boxers. Not that he expected any visitors at this hour, but he'd slung on a pair of comfy pyjama bottoms before going downstairs just in case. Adam had texted earlier to let him know they'd set off. Felix checked his watch. It should take them about three hours to get to him, so they'd arrive around ten o'clock. That gave him about forty minutes to have breakfast and get dressed.

Five minutes after sitting down at the kitchen table with a mug of tea and brown toast, he heard a car pulling up in front. He groaned. Who the hell wanted him at this hour? Just as well he'd put on some clothes, because the doorbell rang a few seconds later.

It was too early to be Adam and Nick, and that didn't leave many people likely to visit him. He had a feeling he knew who it would be before he opened the door. And sure enough, Jamie stood on the other side. Jamie's mouth fell open as Felix leaned against the door frame.

Jamie's gaze swept down over Felix's bare chest and lingered on the tattoo on his right pec before snapping up again. Felix had got it five years ago: four soldiers in silhouette. It was one of his favourites. "Um." Jamie swallowed and started again. "Sorry it's so early. I've been awake ages and didn't realise the time until I got over here."

Jamie's cheeks flushed pink as his gaze dropped again, as though he couldn't help himself. Warmth flared in Felix's belly. It had been a while since he'd been so openly admired. He grinned and raised an eyebrow.

Instead of getting embarrassed as Felix expected, Jamie stood up straighter and shrugged. "If you answer the door like that, then what do you expect?"

Fair enough. At least that cleared up whether Jamie would be interested or not. Felix had no intention of acting on it, but it was good to know. Good for his ego, anyway. He glanced at his watch as Jamie regarded him expectantly, clearly waiting for Felix to invite him in. Which he would have done on any other day, but his mates would be here in about twenty minutes, and the last thing he wanted was for them to meet Jamie. Christ, they'd have a field day.

He didn't want to be rude, but—

"Can I come in?" Jamie smiled then, a real smile that reached his eyes. It lit up his entire face and he looked so much younger.

It caught Felix off guard, and he found himself nodding and stepping back to let Jamie get past.

"Thanks." Jamie ducked his head and he squeezed by. His shoulder rubbed against Felix's bare skin and the rough material of his jacket brushed Felix's right nipple, making him hiss. "Sorry."

Jamie glanced up, meeting Felix's gaze, then down to where they were still touching. The air crackled with tension. Felix felt it down to his toes.

"It's fine." Loose-fitting pyjamas were not the best thing to be wearing at a time like this, and Jamie stood with his hand dangerously close to Felix's groin. If he didn't move soon, things might get interesting.

Fortunately, or unfortunately, depending on which way you looked at it, Jamie carried on walking towards the kitchen-diner area. Felix leaned against the wall and let his head rest back on it. *Fuck.*

He needed to get himself under control. It might have been a while since he'd got any action, but this was ridiculous. Adjusting himself didn't help matters. As soon as he touched his cock, he couldn't resist palming it a couple of times. He should have taken care of his morning wood when he got up.

He sighed. The bulge was there for all to see, but he wasn't about to dash upstairs and change. Jamie could deal with it. That thought brought a smile to his face.

He was still grinning as he entered the kitchen to find Jamie filling the kettle.

"Do you want a cuppa?" Jamie faced the other way as he spoke, only turning to Felix after he'd put the kettle on. He gestured at the half-empty cup on the table. "That's probably cold by now."

Felix leaned on the counter. The movement pushed his hips forward and caught Jamie's eye. "Yeah, if you're making one. Thanks." He watched in amusement as Jamie looked down at the beginnings of Felix's semi.

Jamie turned back to the kettle as it came to the boil, and didn't comment.

"Milk and sugar?" The roughness in Jamie's voice sent a shiver through Felix, but he didn't call him on it.

"Just milk, thanks." They were obviously ignoring whatever this was, and that was fine with

Felix. A little harmless flirting was fun, but taking it further wasn't an option. His phone started to ring as Jamie set a mug of tea on the counter next to him. "Sorry, I need to get this." Jamie gestured for him to go ahead, and Felix answered on the third ring. "Hello?"

"Have you not put me in your bloody contacts yet? What do you do all day now that you're retired?"

"I am not retired, for fuck's sake." Felix huffed out a laugh and moved to sit at the table, taking his tea with him. "Where are you, anyway?"

"Lost. We think Adam missed the turn-off, and we're stuck trying to find somewhere to turn around on these shitty little lanes." Nick paused, and Felix heard Adam swearing up a storm in the background. "Why do you live in the middle of nowhere?"

Felix laughed at him. "It's not that bad. Describe where you are, and I'll direct you back."

Eventually Felix managed to work out where they were and give them instructions on how to get to the cottage. Jamie joined him at the table, and Felix sighed in resignation. His mates would arrive in about five minutes, and Jamie didn't look like he was leaving. Short of Felix physically kicking him out, Jamie was about to meet Adam and Nick with Felix only half dressed.

This should be fun.

"So." Felix drummed his fingers on the table. "I've got guests arriving shortly."

Jamie snorted and glanced pointedly at Felix's phone. "Yes, I gathered that from the directions you gave them."

Felix rolled his eyes. He'd liked to see Jamie still so cocky when two Army sergeants got hold of him. The ribbing Jamie would get wouldn't be half as bad as what they'd give Felix, though. Not that he couldn't give it back just as well, but there were two of them. Should he warn Jamie that his mates were in the services? Nah.

Felix smiled and drank his tea. "Was there a reason you're here so early?" He'd meant to ask before, but Nick's call had interrupted him.

Jamie sat up and rested his arms on the table. "Sort of." He shifted in his seat, looking uncomfortable. Felix was instantly wary. "It can wait until later, though." He glanced out the kitchen window, but there was no sign of a car yet.

Felix shook his head. "They'll probably get lost again, so you might as well start telling me whatever it is." Maybe he should have taken Jamie's easy out and asked him to come back later. But if he stopped and thought about it, he didn't want Jamie to go, despite the shit he'd get when his mates arrived.

"I went back to the police station yesterday." Jamie glanced down at his hands. He hunched his shoulders and all the sparkle from moments earlier seemed to drain out of him.

Felix knew he'd made the right decision. The last thing Jamie needed was to be on his own right then. "To pick up Michael's things?"

"Yeah. They called me first thing and asked me to come in." He took a drink of his tea before continuing. "But that's not what I wanted to talk to you about."

"Oh?"

"I asked them if anyone had seen Michael the day he disappeared."

Felix had an idea where Jamie was going with this: The police had interviewed Felix after he gave his statement. "And they mentioned me?"

Jamie nodded. "Yep. I knew someone had seen his car on the beach road, but I didn't know it was you until today." He leaned back in his chair. "The police seem a lot more forthcoming than they were before." He played with the handle on his mug and glanced up at Felix expectantly.

Felix sighed. Now would be a good time for his mates to arrive. He didn't want to get into this with Jamie, but the hopeful and slightly desperate expression on Jamie's face was that of a man with no idea what to think or where to get the answers he needed. It pulled at Felix; an uncomfortable tightness in his chest caused the words to tumble out. "He was there earlier than normal that day. Michael, I mean."

The sun suddenly made an appearance, shining through the kitchen window, and the glare forced Felix to change position before continuing. "I pass that beach at least a couple of times each day, and I'd never seen his car there before eleven. Usually it was after lunch, and I remember thinking he must have got up early."

Jamie hummed. A small smile curved his lips. "Sounds like him." Felix raised an eyebrow, so Jamie elaborated. "He gets caught up in things—painting, reading, whatever he happens to be doing at the time. Goes to sleep late, gets up late."

"All right for some," Felix muttered without thinking, and immediately regretted it at the look of despair on Jamie's face. Clearly things hadn't ended all right for Michael. "Sorry."

Jamie waved him away. "It's fine." He even managed another smile. "He's always been a bit of a lazy arse in the morning."

The conversation halted. Jamie had a wistful glint to his eye, obviously remembering something Felix wasn't privy to. Just as Felix relaxed and thought they were done talking about it, Jamie cocked his head to one side, his gaze narrowing.

"Why do you pass that stretch of road so often? Do your aunt and uncle have other properties over that way?"

Felix opened his mouth and stopped, unsure how to answer that. Yes, they did have a cottage a mile or so past Weston's house, but that wasn't the reason. Jamie had been so forthcoming and honest that Felix had the urge to be the same way. "Yes, my aunt owns another property farther along that road, but—"

The rev of an engine followed by the crunch of gravel saved him from explaining further, but Felix couldn't decide whether to be relieved or disappointed. Now was not the time to dwell on it. He stood and watched both car doors open at the same time, helpless to do anything but grin as Adam and Nick unfolded themselves out of the small car they'd pulled up in.

Two grown men, both well over six foot tall and built, climbing out of a smart car wasn't a sight you saw every day.

Forgetting all about Jamie, Felix marched towards the front door and pulled it open. He watched them haul their bags out of the tiny boot.

"What the fuck is that thing?" He laughed and gestured to the dark blue car now parked between his Audi and Jamie's Honda. Jamie's car wasn't that much bigger, but Felix's made the smart car look like a toy. "I'm surprised you both fit inside, let alone got it to move."

Adam grinned back and walked towards him, his bag hefted over one shoulder. "You can talk, you fat bastard. Going soft now you're a civvy?" He slapped Felix hard on the belly, the sound loud as his hand met bare skin, before pulling Felix into a tight hug. "Christ, it's good to see you."

"You too," Felix gritted out. He hunched into the embrace, flinching as the rough material of Adam's jacket rubbed against his now-stinging skin. Maybe he *was* getting soft. Trying not to bring attention to it, he hugged Adam back and patted him on the back of the head, making sure to be just as rough. Adam laughed at him and ducked away. "And fuck you, I am not fat." Felix made a point of tensing his muscles and patting his stomach. He still had a great six-pack, so they could fuck right off. "You're just jealous. I've been out for two months and still look better than you tossers."

Someone cleared their throat behind him. Felix glanced over his shoulder to see Jamie standing awkwardly in the entranceway. His gaze flitted to Felix's hand where it rested low on his belly, then up to Adam's face before finally meeting Felix's eyes. "So... I'm gonna head out."

Adam and Nick glanced at Jamie, then back to Felix—two sets of eyes taking in his half-dressed appearance with new insight and jumping to totally the wrong conclusion. Felix groaned inwardly.

Jamie took a step forward, which brought him almost within touching distance. He frowned when Felix didn't move away from the door frame, and nodded over at his car. "Can I get past?" His gaze darted down to Felix's bare chest, lingering on his tattoo again.

Adam snorted, and Jamie flushed at being caught in the act.

"Come on, ladies. Are we going inside or what?" Nick's booming voice made both Felix and Jamie jump. Felix hadn't been barked at that loudly in a while. "I'm bloody dying for a piss and a cuppa."

Felix glanced back at Jamie and shrugged. With Adam and Nick standing in front of the door, the only way for Jamie to get out was for them to move. Judging by the way they didn't so much as offer to step back, coupled with their gleeful expressions, Jamie was going nowhere.

Felix turned and faced him. "Fancy another cuppa?"

Jamie started to shake his head and gesture to his car; he even had his keys out ready. "I really should—"

"Nonsense." Adam gave Felix a light shove, almost pushing him into Jamie and forcing Jamie to take a couple of steps back towards the kitchen. "No need to leave on our account." He shot Felix a suggestive look and grinned widely. "Felix has always had shitty manners. I bet he's not even offered you breakfast."

Jamie opened his mouth but no words came out. He looked to Felix, as if willing him to jump in any minute, but Felix knew from painful experience that it was pointless to try and argue.

Adam carried on, already sensing victory. "It's the least he can do after keeping you up all night." He winked at Jamie, and Jamie flushed.

"I'm not.... We didn't...." He looked as though the floor couldn't swallow him up quickly enough.

All of a sudden, Adam seemed to realise he'd got it wrong. Not that it made any difference. If anything, his expression turned even more gleeful at the thought of embarrassing them. "My mistake."

He didn't budge, and Jamie slumped his shoulders, accepting defeat. He turned around and headed back into the kitchen. Adam squeezed past, shoulder-barging Felix on his way.

"Losing your touch, Bergie?" Nick pulled him into a hug of his own. The familiarity of it sent a pang of longing through Felix so sharp his breath caught. Fuck, he'd missed them. "A few years ago you'd have had him worn out and begging for more by now. Slowing down in your old age?"

"Fuck off," Felix replied at the same time as Jamie's pained "I can still hear you, you know!" floated into the doorway.

Nick grinned as he stepped back, clasping Felix's shoulder hard before turning and following after Adam.

Oh God. Felix let his head fall back against the wall and closed his eyes for a second. He imagined the scene unfolding in the next room and couldn't decide whether to leave them to it or go rescue Jamie. At least they'd take Jamie's mind off his brother for a while if nothing else.

With a resigned sigh, Felix pushed off the wall and followed them all into the kitchen.

Chapter Seven

Jamie leaned against the counter in Felix's kitchen, wishing he were anywhere else but there and wondering if anyone would stop him if he tried to run. He'd never thought of himself as small before, but standing next to these two men made him feel that way.

They stood on either side of him, regarding him with open curiosity. Even dressed in jeans and jackets, the way they held themselves screamed military. He should have known Felix's guests would be Army men.

"So." The guy on his right eyed him like a cat peering down at a juicy plump mouse. "Felix is fucking useless on all fronts." He ignored Felix's shout of protest from the hallway and held out his hand. "We'll introduce ourselves, shall we? I'm Nick." He shook Jamie's hand and then gestured to the guy next to him. "And this is Adam."

Jamie reached past Nick and shook Adam's hand too as Felix appeared in the kitchen doorway.

Felix rolled his eyes and wandered over to stand in front of the three of them. "At least I know how to do introductions properly, not half-arsed ones like that." Felix met Jamie's gaze and flashed him a warm smile.

Jamie's stomach fluttered. Heat spread up through his chest and he automatically smiled back. He wanted to kick himself—he didn't like Felix, and he didn't trust him. A charming smile and a bare chest weren't going to change that.

"Jamie Matthews, meet Sergeant Adam Smith and Colour Sergeant Nick Taylor. I had the dubious pleasure of serving with these two arseholes for the last twelve years."

Jamie smiled and nodded in acknowledgment.

Felix turned back to him and carried on talking. "Jamie's staying in one of my aunt's cottages." He looked pointedly at Nick, and Jamie watched as Nick's face went through several different expressions, finally settling on sheepish.

"Shit." Nick rubbed the back of his neck. "Sorry about earlier. I didn't realise you were a guest."

Jamie wondered whether to say anything further when it became clear Felix wasn't going to give any more explanation than that. He wasn't exactly a normal paying guest, and they hadn't offended him.

He could let them stew for a bit, though. Payback.

The ensuing silence edged into uncomfortable territory and threatened awkwardness all around. There'd been enough of that already, so Jamie decided to clear the air. It wasn't as though they wouldn't ask about him as soon as he left, anyway.

He drew in a deep breath. "Don't worry about it. I'm not on holiday or anything. My brother rented the cottage, but he went missing a week last Saturday, presumed drowned." A couple of pairs of raised eyebrows met his declaration, the timing so in sync that Jamie had to stifle a bubble of inappropriate laughter. "I've come down to collect his things and to see if the police have any more information."

Nick glanced from Jamie to Felix and then back again. Jamie expected the usual "I'm sorry" or "how awful," and he tensed, waiting for them.

"Did the police have anything else to tell you?" Nick asked, taking Jamie by surprise.

Jamie couldn't stop himself from looking at Felix first. No one missed it.

Adam straightened up and crossed his arms. "What the fuck's going on?" Although his voice wasn't raised, his tone brooked no argument. Jamie had no trouble imagining him barking out orders and having people jump to carry them out.

Felix groaned and glanced up at the ceiling before catching Jamie's eye with a sort of "can I tell them your story?" look.

Jamie nodded — go ahead. He'd been through it so many times now, the last thing he wanted was to explain it all again.

"Fine." Felix turned, took a step towards the living room, then looked back over his shoulder. "Come on, then, I'm not explaining everything standing up in the bloody kitchen."

Jamie trooped through after him, with Adam and Nick close behind. The living room was bigger than Jamie expected. Two large sofas positioned at right angles to each other filled the space, facing a large TV in the corner. Felix took a seat on the nearest sofa, and Jamie followed suit, sinking into the soft-looking cushions.

Adam and Nick took the other sofa. Both sat forward and propped their elbows on their knees.

Jamie had the urge to ask if they did everything in sync, like swimmers. The thought made him snort in amusement, causing everyone to focus on him. He ducked his head, and made a show of sorting out his laces. What the hell was wrong with him? Glancing at Felix to get his mind back to the present, Jamie cursed silently. Focusing would be a lot easier to do if Felix put a shirt on.

He kept his gaze on Felix's face, refusing to let it stray again as Felix began to tell Adam and Nick about Michael and his disappearance. Jamie chipped in here and there to add bits to the story or correct something Felix got wrong. On the whole he explained everything much more clearly and concisely than Jamie would have done. Jamie guessed it was easier when the missing person wasn't a member of your family.

"...So there you have it."

Jamie settled back into the soft cushions.

Nick met his gaze. "Forgive me for being blunt. I understand what a difficult time this is for you, but what does Felix have to do with all of this? I get the feeling there's more to it than being a concerned landlord."

That's what I'd like to know too.

Maybe the arrival of Felix's friends would prove to be more fruitful than Jamie imagined. A frisson of excitement ran through him at the prospect of finally getting some information out of Felix.

"Felix?" Adam reached out and kicked Felix in the shin, making him wince and scoot his leg out of the way. "Stop pissing about and explain."

Jamie sat forward, almost on the edge of his seat, jittery with anticipation.

Felix bit his lip, looking uncertain for once. "You know how I said I was the one to spot Michael's car on the beach road that day? How I'd seen it there most days before that?"

"Yeah?" Nick said, and Adam nodded.

"Well, there's a house that overlooks that beach." Felix paused as though the gravity of the situation was too much for him, and Jamie clenched his fists, willing him to spit it out already. "It's owned by Karl Weston."

He stopped there, and Jamie frowned. Was that it? He glanced over at Nick and Adam, who wore matching looks of recognition. Clearly, Jamie was missing something. A *big* something.

"Westie?" Adam asked. Felix nodded. "Why the fuck would he buy a house here? I mean, as nice as the area is...?"

"I know."

"And why were you driving by it every day? Because I very much doubt that you passing the road Westie's house is on happens to be a fucking coincidence. What have you done, Felix?"

Jamie's gaze ping-ponged between them as they carried on speaking as though they'd forgotten he was there.

Felix sighed and focused on his clasped hands. "Nothing."

"Bollocks." Adam stood and walked over to the picture windows at the back of the room. They overlooked rolling fields and stone walls, and Jamie admired the view for a second until Felix sighed again, capturing his attention.

"I've been watching his house."

"Jesus Christ," Adam muttered at the same time as Nick's "What the fuck for?"

Nick turned and stalked over to stand in front of Felix, towering over him where Felix remained seated, his head in his hands. "I'm telling you this as your friend, Felix. You need to let this thing with

Weston go. What happened to Jason was fucking awful. I know you think Weston had something to do with it—"

Felix's head snapped up at that. "You both agreed the whole bloody thing was suspicious."

"Suspicious, yes, but there was no evidence that pointed to Weston at the time. What can you possibly hope to achieve by watching his fucking house now? Apart from getting yourself arrested. For fuck's sake, Felix."

Jamie's head spun as he listened to them shout at each other. He knew there was more to Felix's story than he'd let on. "Would someone please explain what you're talking about?"

Everyone turned to stare at him and Jamie squirmed uncomfortably. Being on the end of a look that intense was bad enough from one person, let alone three of them. Felix's stare had a touch of surprise mixed in, as though he'd not expected Jamie to still be there. And to be honest, Jamie was starting to wish he was somewhere else.

"I'm going to put the kettle on and make a brew." Nick pointed at Felix, jabbing his finger in the air. "You explain to Jamie about your obsession with Karl Weston. When I get back, you can then explain what the hell this has to do with a missing person, because your interest in this"—he nodded in Jamie's direction—"is not a fucking coincidence."

The room fell silent and all three of them watched Nick walk out.

Adam let out a harsh breath and shot an apologetic glance Felix's way. "It's been a bitch of a month."

Felix nodded in understanding.

Jamie's blood chilled at the implications of that statement. Maybe he should leave. Whatever connection Felix had to Karl Weston was none of Jamie's business, and he doubted it had anything to do with Michael's disappearance. According to the police, Weston hadn't even been at the house on the Saturday that Michael vanished. He rose to go, but a firm hand on his wrist stopped him in his tracks. When he glanced down, Felix was staring up at him.

"Where are you going?" Felix frowned and nodded back at the sofa. "Don't you want to hear this?"

The warmth from where Felix touched him sent tingles up Jamie's spine. Even though his grip was loose, Jamie felt the strength there. If Felix wanted to keep him there, Jamie would be powerless to stop him — which was more appealing than it should have been.

Jamie swallowed thickly and hoped his voice wouldn't betray his thoughts. "I don't think this concerns me anymore. I'm sure you and your friends have things to catch up on."

"For fuck's sake, just tell him!" Nick yelled from the kitchen before Felix had a chance to answer.

Felix gave a gentle tug on Jamie's wrist, urging him back down. "Come on. It might explain what I was looking for at your cottage."

His curiosity getting the better of him, Jamie sat down. "Okay." He made himself comfy, settling back into the deep sofa cushion. This wouldn't be a quick story. The resigned and wistful expression that Felix now wore told him it wouldn't be a happy one either.

"Jason joined the Army at the same time as me and Karl Weston. We all went through basic training together and ended up in the same regiment. Weston left as soon as the required four years were up—"

"And good fucking riddance." Nick appeared at the entrance to the living room, carrying two mugs of tea. "The bloke turned out to be a right wanker." He passed one mug to Adam and the other to Felix, then returned to the kitchen.

"As I was saying, he left and no one heard from him again." With a wry smile, Felix's gaze met Adam's. "Because he turned out to be a right wanker." Adam snorted into his tea. "Except for Jason. For God knows what reason, Jason got on okay with him, and must have kept in touch because that's the first place he went when he left the Army last year."

"To see Weston?" Jamie accepted a mug of tea when Nick appeared with two more. "Thanks."

Nick nodded and sat down.

"Yeah." Felix sighed, and then fixed Jamie with a dark look. "How much do you know about Weston?"

Jamie took a sip of his tea before answering. "I googled him."

"I thought you might." Felix grinned, but his smile was fleeting. "There's not much on him, is there?"

"No." Jamie shook his head. "Surprisingly little."

"Even with all the success he seems to have enjoyed since leaving the Army, he's managed to keep himself squeaky clean and out of the papers."

As much as Jamie wanted to hear the rest of the story, the journalist in him couldn't help but challenge Felix's remark. "And what makes you think he isn't 'squeaky clean.' Just because you think the guy's a wanker doesn't make him a criminal." He ignored Felix's indignant huff. "Isn't it equally possible that he just worked really hard?"

Felix tensed. Adam's groan from across the room implied he knew what was coming next and had heard it all before. Many times.

"He may have worked hard, but I don't think for one second it was within the law."

Excitement stirred Jamie's blood. It had been a while since he'd had the chance to challenge someone like this, and he smiled despite the seriousness of the conversation topic. "What makes you say that?"

"Karl Weston left the Army at twenty-two years old, with a vague idea about 'making it' in London. He had no fucking idea what to do with himself, yet three years later he's sending Jason pictures of his new flat in Central London and telling him all about the string of properties he's going to buy." Felix stopped and picked up his mug.

Jamie's gaze wandered to Felix's hands where they rested atop his knees holding the mug steady. "Do you know what he did in those three years?"

Felix had big strong-looking hands and thick fingers. His arms were well toned and covered in fine dark hairs, and Jamie followed the way the muscles moved as Felix brought the mug to his mouth and took a drink. And that brought Jamie's gaze in line with his bare chest and that damn tattoo. He had resisted looking at that while they'd been sitting, but it drew his eyes now.

Felix cleared his throat and Jamie's eyes snapped up. *Shit.*

Felix didn't comment on Jamie's obvious staring, but Jamie felt the heat in his gaze like a burn. Felix kept eye contact, daring Jamie to look away first. "When I asked Jason about it, he said Weston had made some good connections and knew the right people. He didn't elaborate and I didn't ask. I didn't give a shit if Weston was doing something illegal or not. He wasn't my problem. Not then, anyway."

Jamie struggled to find his voice under the weight of Felix's stare, but his curiosity won out over whatever else was going on in his head, and he managed, "What changed?"

"We came back from Afghanistan, and Jason decided enough was enough. He was done. By then Weston had a string of properties across London, and he offered one to Jason while he got himself sorted."

"What's so bad about that?" Jamie prompted.

Felix scoffed and slumped back against the cushions.

When he looked up at the ceiling, Jamie immediately felt the loss of his gaze on him. He shrugged it off and tried to regain some composure.

"Jason was in a good position financially when he left the Army, and he had good job prospects — at least five interviews waiting for him when he got out. I warned him off Weston, reminded him what a twat he was, but Jason knew better. Said Weston had changed since we knew him. What a crock of shit." He turned his head to face Jamie. "Jason had a..." Felix turned away again and closed his eyes, but not before Jamie caught the haunted look in them. He covered his face with his hands. "Fuck."

When Felix made no effort to move, Adam continued the story. "Jason had a weakness for gambling. I think that's one reason his parents encouraged him to join up in the first place. To get him away from all that. We only knew because Jason told us about it, said the Army had been the best thing that could have happened to him. It wasn't a problem while he served, but when he got out—"

"Karl Weston introduced him to a lifestyle he couldn't afford. And you can imagine what happened then."

Jamie swallowed past the lump in his throat. Next to him, Felix practically vibrated with restrained anger, and Jamie hesitated to say anything that might grate on him further. But he also looked like he needed to get this out. Jamie guessed, "He started gambling."

"Yep." Felix exhaled slowly and the tension seemed to drain away along with it. His voice was surprisingly soft when he spoke again. "I told him to leave, told him to go stay with my parents—they cared about Jason almost as much as I did—and we'd help him sort out his debt. But I refused to give him any money until he got away from that arsehole. Shit. If I'd only—" His breath caught and he sat up suddenly, resting his head in his hands.

Jamie glanced over at Nick and Adam, eyebrows raised in question, although he was pretty sure he knew what was coming next.

Nick sighed. His gaze was full of concern as he looked at Felix's hunched shoulders. "Jason got himself in a big fucking hole, too deep to get out. He called all of us, begging for money, and we would have given it to him in a second if he'd agreed to stop gambling and get out of London. But he refused, and no way were we going to give him more money to piss away, so we said no." He glanced over at Felix again and shook his head sadly. "We wanted to help him, but not like that. He needed to get away from that lifestyle, and if he couldn't do it himself, then we would. We were on our way down there when we found out."

Oh fuck. Jamie thought back to the conversation he'd had with Felix earlier that week. *"Jason called me two days before he died. We argued, and I told him he was a fucking idiot and hung up."* Christ.

Felix scrubbed his hands over his face and looked up, gaze intent on Nick and Adam. "We had leave that weekend. Three days off to get down to London, talk some sense into him, and get him out of there. We were going to work on how to fix his debt problem as soon as we got him away. But he'd never let on how bad it was, or what kind of people he'd borrowed money from. Not until that last phone call."

Jamie wasn't stupid, he could put all the pieces together without them having to spell it out. But it all sounded a bit far-fetched. Surely things like that didn't happened in real life? "So you think the burglary was faked." He shifted in his seat, drawing one leg up and twisting to face Felix. "You think... what, that Karl Weston killed Jason because he couldn't pay?"

"No, for fuck's sake. He's not a fucking mob boss," Felix snapped, and Jamie stared back at him because that was exactly what he'd implied. "Jason said he'd had a couple of threats from the people he owed. People that Weston introduced him to. He'd laughed them off, saying he could handle himself. I told him to be careful, and I knew he was scared but wouldn't admit it. We argued and he ended the call."

Felix hung his head again and absently waved at Nick to carry on for him.

"Jason lived in a posh flat, but he had nothing left to steal in it. The police suggested the burglars probably wouldn't have known that, even if they were coming to collect on his debts. They probably assumed he had something worth money, considering the address of the flat. The police said that when Jason disturbed them, they must have fought and he died—fell head first onto a granite coffee table and never regained consciousness."

The room lapsed into silence. Jamie's head swam with all the information they'd thrown at him. But as awful as Jason's story was, he wasn't convinced they were right to blame Weston for it, or what any of it had to do with Michael. Michael had never gambled in his life, and he did all right for money. He didn't have loads, but as far as Jamie was aware, he didn't have any debt either, not even a student loan.

Not wanting to piss anyone off but feeling like the question needed to be asked, Jamie said, "How can you be sure that Weston had anything to do with it?"

Felix laughed nastily and shook his head. "Weston turned up at the funeral, saying how gutted he was that something so terrible had happened to Jason in a property that he owned. He said he felt responsible, and I fucking knew he'd had something to do with it. His voice was sincere enough, but you could see it in his eyes. He wanted me to know that he'd done it and there wasn't a bloody thing we could do to prove it."

"Did you go to the police?" Jamie fiddled with the laces on his trainers as the tension in the room rose again. The subject was clearly still a touchy one for Felix, though not as much for the others, he noticed, and he needed to tread carefully.

"Yeah, but there was nothing they could do. They questioned Weston, since he'd been one of the last people to talk to Jason. But they had nothing to connect him to Jason's gambling debts, and Weston had an alibi for that night. Of fucking course he did. So they politely told me to go back to Warminster and let them do their jobs. And that was eleven months ago."

Nick let out a heavy sigh from across the room. "Which is why you need to let it drop. Karl Weston is a piece of shit but untouchable as far as Jason's death is concerned." He sent a steely look Felix's way. "Stop wasting your time on that bastard. He's not worth the effort." He looked pointedly at him until Felix gave the barest of nods. "About fucking time."

Jamie sat there feeling like an intruder in what had turned into a very personal moment between three friends. He didn't know Jason, couldn't appreciate the pain the three of them had been through together with his death, let alone all the other shit they must have seen with all the time they served in the Army. But despite all that, he still didn't get what any of this had to do with Michael. He had no connection to Karl Weston other than he went missing from the beach overlooked by Weston's house. An odd coincidence, yes, but it would take a lot more than that to convince Jamie that Weston was somehow involved in Michael's disappearance.

Loath as he was to bring the subject up, Felix had promised him an explanation. "What were you searching for that day at the cottage?" Felix glanced over at him, saying nothing for several seconds until Jamie began to get uncomfortable. "Michael had only been down here a little over a week, and he never mentioned meeting anyone. What makes you think he even knew Weston owned the house, let alone ever met him?"

"Michael met me, but he never told you that either," Felix countered.

Adam stood and walked over to the picture windows. He hadn't said much since they'd been in the living room, and Jamie wondered what he and Nick thought to all of this. They'd come down expecting an easy day catching up with Felix, and instead Jamie had appeared, dragging up old, painful memories. They must hate him.

"Jamie's got a point, Felix." Adam said, surprising him. "I know you hate Weston. We all do, and for good reason. But just because he's here doesn't mean he's involved this time." He rubbed at the back of his head, scraping his fingers over his short hair. "Let's get this shit sorted out and then we can have a fucking drink. I think we'll need one."

Jamie glanced at his watch: a touch after eleven thirty in the morning. A little early to start drinking, but Adam was right. The intensity of the last hour or so made it feel like late afternoon already. He sighed and glanced at Felix, and the weight of the situation settled on his shoulders again. For a while he'd not been thinking about Michael, too caught up in Felix's story about Jason, but now it all came back with a vengeance. "I just want to know why you think Michael and Weston are connected. That's all."

Felix looked at him, and his piercing blue eyes pinned Jamie to the spot. "Because he's a shady motherfucker. Because according to my aunt he uses that house twice a month at the most, yet for the last two weeks he's spent the best part of eight days there. Something changed. Something happened to keep him here, and my gut tells me that it has everything to do with your brother's disappearance." He sighed again and looked away.

Jamie blinked rapidly at the loss of eye contact, cursing himself for getting so wrapped up in Felix's attention again.

Adam turned back from the window and glared at the back of Felix's head. "Is that why you were watching him? Because you thought you might see Michael?" Felix must have felt it because a second or two later he swivelled in his seat to look over at him. "I don't mean to be insensitive—" Adam glanced briefly at Jamie. "—but if Weston is involved, I doubt he'd leave anything incriminating at the house."

The obvious "like a dead body" went unsaid, but Jamie knew they were all thinking it. The pain was sharp and immediate, and he bit back the automatic "he's not fucking dead" threatening to spill out.

"I know that," Felix snapped back, not looking Jamie's way.

Adam held his hands out, palms up. "Then what the fuck were you hoping to see? Westie's not a moron, and it's not like you can watch his house round the clock. If he did kill him, and I'm being purely bloody hypothetical here, then he's hardly likely to conveniently haul out a dead body in the middle of the day for you to see. What the fuck would he do with it?"

And that was it. Jamie shot to his feet and left the room without another word. If they wanted to believe his brother was dead, then fine. He understood all the evidence pointed to that fact, and he didn't blame people for drawing that conclusion. He could handle that. What he couldn't cope with, and refused to sit and fucking listen to, was the two of them talking about his brother like that. As though he were nothing more than some inconvenient *thing* to be disposed of.

As he shoved open the front door, he heard Nick's voice coming from the living room.

"Nicely done, you tactless pair of dicks."

Chapter Eight

"Fuck." Felix let his head fall into his hands as the front door slammed. The sound echoed loudly in the now-silent living room. He stood to go after Jamie, feeling like the biggest arsehole ever.

Nick raised an eyebrow at him as he passed. "So it *is* like that, then?"

"Fuck off." Felix stalked past him without another word, ignoring the soft huff of laughter behind him.

He got to the door and stopped, with his fingers wrapped around the door handle. What the hell did he say now? "Sorry for talking about your dead brother like he was a slab of meat"? It sounded shitty in his head, let alone out loud. He didn't know Jamie well enough to gauge what he'd meet on the other side of that door. At least Jamie was still out there. No car had started up, so he hadn't left yet.

Felix steeled himself for a very pissed-off Jamie and opened the front door.

Jamie stood about ten feet away, facing out towards the fields with his back to Felix. He made no move to show he'd heard him come out. Not that Felix expected him to.

"I'm sorry about that just now." He took a couple of steps closer. "It was a shitty way to talk about your brother."

Jamie's shoulders rose and fell as though he'd taken a huge deep breath and let it out, probably attempting to calm down before he spoke. Felix appreciated the effort, doubting he would have bothered if he'd been in Jamie's position. "Yeah, it was."

It came out rough, as if he'd forced it out through gritted teeth. Not calm at all, then.

Felix bridged the rest of the distance between them until he stood alongside him. The green and yellow fields of his aunt and uncle's property stretched out before them, the farmhouse visible from where they were. In Felix's experience, when a person felt that full of anger and hurt, it was best to let it out; Felix had been there.

He suspected Jamie hadn't done that yet — yelled and screamed about how fucking unfair all this was. And if Felix had to be the person he dumped it all on, then so be it. He had thick skin, and he felt partly responsible for making it worse. "Hey." He nudged Jamie with his shoulder, wanting to provoke a reaction.

He got one.

Jamie's head snapped towards him so fast that Felix winced, thinking Jamie must have strained something. "What the hell is wrong with you? You poke your nose into my business, search through my brother's things, for fuck's sake, as if it's your bloody right. And what the fuck for? All because you have some axe to grind with Karl Weston." He sucked in a harsh breath but didn't appear finished by any means. Felix stayed quiet, letting him rant. "I told you I checked with the police. Weston wasn't even here on that Saturday. He left for London late Friday night. He has witnesses. So please tell me how he managed to be in two places at once? I'm all ears." His eyes flashed, full of sadness and anger, and Felix felt a sympathetic ache in his chest. He knew how much it hurt. "We don't even know for sure that Michael's dead."

"Jamie." Felix kept his voice soft. "If someone didn't kill him, and he didn't drown in the sea, then where is he?"

"I—"

Jamie looked so lost. Felix saw the exact moment he considered the fact that his brother was actually dead. The anger melted away as Jamie struggled to find words, leaving only despair in its place. "I don't know," he whispered.

Felix moved on instinct, bringing his hands up to cup Jamie's face and draw him in. Maybe it was his stricken expression or the way his voice broke a little at the end, but Felix found himself closing the last of the small space between them. His lips brushed Jamie's, a soft kiss meant to comfort or distract; Felix had no idea what he was doing. He let the touch linger for a second, aware of Jamie standing frozen, and not wanting to push him into anything.

Jamie's lips were soft and warm, and the temptation to tease them open with his tongue was hard to ignore, but Jamie was either shocked or horrified, because he hadn't moved. Then, as Felix went to pull away, Jamie gripped him by the hips, anchoring him in place, and finally kissed him back.

Felix gasped, surprised by the force of it, and Jamie took the opportunity to deepen the kiss. There was nothing gentle or comforting about it anymore. Jamie clung to him, his mouth rough and desperate as he slipped his arms around Felix and backed him up against the side of his car. He worked a thigh between Felix's legs, making Felix's breath hitch.

Up close, Jamie smelled freshly showered, with faint traces of something citrusy clinging to his skin. He must have shaved that morning, because Felix felt nothing but smoothness under his hands. Jamie moaned and pressed his hips into Felix's, creating a delicious friction as he pinned him against the rear passenger door. The handle dug into Felix's backside, but he ignored it in favour of thrusting back against Jamie, flinching when the cold metal of Jamie's belt buckle touched his belly. This was not how he'd imagined his morning going, but he wasn't about to complain.

When Jamie eventually pulled back, breathing heavily, he met Felix's gaze with a mixture of heat and confusion. "Why did you do that?"

Felix let out a breathy laugh and rubbed at his lips with a thumb. "Hey, I might've started it, but you did the rest." He gestured at their current position, with Felix still leaning against Jamie's car and Jamie plastered against him from the waist down. He let his hands slide and gripped the top of Jamie's shoulders. "Not that I'm complaining."

They stared at each other for a couple of seconds before Jamie looked down between them and scoffed. "I don't even like you."

Despite the gravity of the conversation only minutes before, Felix was helpless to stop himself shifting his hips. The telltale hardness in Jamie's jeans made him smile. "I beg to differ."

Jamie glanced back up and shrugged. A small answering smile appeared on his lips. "It's only a semi."

"It was only a kiss." Felix's grin widened, and he rubbed his thumbs along Jamie's collarbone. "Imagine what would happen if I—"

The loud ringtone of Jamie's phone startled them both, and Jamie immediately stepped back out of Felix's embrace and pulled his phone out of his pocket. Felix let his hands fall to his sides, and groaned. Just when things were getting interesting.

"Sorry." Jamie frowned at his phone, glancing up briefly to catch Felix's gaze. "I need to take it, it's my mum." He answered the phone as he turned and took a few steps away from Felix. Talking quietly to his mum, he walked a little farther until Felix had to strain to make out what he was saying.

Whatever it was, it was none of Felix's business, so with a sigh and a quick adjustment of the bulge in his pyjama bottoms, he left Jamie to it. Once through the front door, Felix paused at the foot of the stairs. His pj's left disturbingly little to the imagination, and walking back into the living room with a still-obvious bulge was asking for trouble. He ought to go and put some clothes on, for everyone's sake.

Five minutes later, after a quick wash and dressed in jeans and a black T-shirt, Felix emerged from his bedroom. He jogged down the stairs to see if Jamie had finished his call and hopefully to intercept him before he went back in to join the others. Felix could do without their impromptu kiss becoming common knowledge. Not that he thought Jamie would divulge anything, but Nick had a habit of noticing everything. It was one of the things that made him such a good leader.

"Oh." Felix stopped in the doorway to the living room when he saw only Adam and Nick in there, sprawled out on the sofa, chatting. They glanced Felix's way, pausing mid-conversation.

"What?"

Felix shook his head. "Nothing. I was expecting Jamie to be in here, that's all."

Adam looked him up and down. "I thought the idea was to lose clothes, not put more on."

"Piss off. I told you it's not li—" Except it was sort of like that now. Maybe? Felix sighed and closed his eyes. What the fuck did he know? "I'll be back in a sec." He didn't bother waiting for a reply, but Adam's laughter and a "Sure you will," followed him out.

Wankers.

When he opened the front door, Felix pulled up short as he spotted Jamie at his car with the driver's door open and a guilty look on his face. "Going somewhere?" He walked over to him, the crunch of gravel loud in the silence.

"I need to go back to the cottage for a while." Jamie bit his lip but held Felix's gaze.

Once again, Felix struggled to read his expression, and a flare of irritation sparked inside him. He tended to get a good read on most people, but for some reason, Jamie kept him guessing. He didn't like it one bit. "Fair enough. A heads-up might have been nice."

"Yeah, sorry. I just—" He waved a hand between the two of them and then at the cottage. "I didn't know if you said anything, and—"

"I didn't."

"Oh."

Felix shoved his hands in his pockets, wondering what to say to get Jamie to stay. After the morning they'd had, the last thing Jamie needed was to go back to that cottage and sit surrounded by his brother's things, but he doubted Jamie would appreciate him putting it like that. "Can I persuade you to stay for lunch?" He smiled and shot Jamie his best come-fuck-me look, gratified when Jamie flushed.

Jamie shook his head and clutched the door frame. "I don't think that's a good idea."

"No?" Felix walked closer until he stood on the other side of the car door. "And why's that?" He'd not thought about taking things further with Jamie until that kiss. Yes, he might have given him an admiring once-over, but actually making plans to get him naked was another thing altogether. But now… now he wanted to see what was under that loose-fitting T-shirt and tight jeans. He wouldn't force Jamie to stay, but a little gentle persuasion never hurt. He reached out and laid a hand on Jamie's, where it clutched the top of the car door. "I thought we were starting to get on well." Felix let his little finger trace over the back of Jamie's hand, the touch slow and feather-light.

Jamie swallowed and carefully withdrew his hand from under Felix's, shaking his head.

Damn. Must be losing my touch.

"You and your friends probably have a lot of catching up to do. I don't want to intrude." He tapped his keys against the top of the car, contemplating something, and then sighed. "Look, to be honest, this morning has been…." He smiled a little and his gaze dropped to Felix's mouth. "Informative." Felix grinned in response, knowing what Jamie was thinking about. "All of it. And I need a bit of space to let it all sink in. Know what I mean?"

Felix stepped back, giving Jamie some space, because yes, he knew exactly what Jamie meant. But he still didn't like the idea of Jamie brooding alone in that cottage all night. "Okay, but why don't you come back later for dinner and a drink?" He nodded over his shoulder at his house and those inside it. "They might seem like a couple of twats, but they're great guys, I promise. Might do you good to unwind a little. Besides, they're going to rip the piss out of me something fierce. You wouldn't want to miss that, would you?"

Finally, Jamie smiled back at him and nodded. "Yeah, okay. Since you put it that way. What time?"

"We'll probably eat around eightish, but come back whenever you like. We'll be here."

Felix watched Jamie nod and duck down inside his car. Was he stupid to want to get involved with Jamie? Probably. Did he care? Fuck no. He waited until Jamie's car disappeared down the drive, and headed back inside.

"Where's Jamie?" Nick looked up at him as soon as Felix entered the living room. They'd moved from the sofa and now sat on the floor leaning back against it, with PS4 controllers in hand.

"Gone home." Felix glanced at the TV screen to see what they were playing and rolled his eyes. Of course. The opening music for *Call of Duty* blared out of the speakers, and Nick's attention snapped back to the screen. "Really?" Felix pointed at the TV when they glanced back at him. "*Black Ops?*"

Nick shrugged. "What else? Go make a cuppa, and then you can watch how it's done."

"Fuck off."

Grinning, Nick waved him off in the direction of the kitchen and turned back around. "And don't think we won't be talking about the Weston thing either."

With a groan, Felix left to go and make tea. He'd hoped they'd have exhausted that topic of conversation. Obviously not. What more was there to say, though? He'd spent countless hours watching Weston and now realised what a colossal waste of time that had been. He didn't need to examine his reasons for doing it in greater detail.

Carrying three mugs of tea at once wasn't the best idea, and Felix hissed as the hot ceramic burnt his fingers. He set them down on the coffee table and sat on the end of the sofa.

"So." Nick shot someone on screen before nudging Felix's knee with his shoulder. "You and Jamie?" Felix laughed as Nick's on-screen character died spectacularly. Nick turned around to jab him in the thigh. "Well?"

"What about us?" Felix fiddled with the seam on his jeans, then flopped back against the sofa.

"When did that happen?"

"There's nothing—" He stopped at Nick's raised eyebrow. "Why are you so interested, anyway?" Talking about each other's respective relationships wasn't something they did a lot of. He knew Nick's wife well enough and had met a couple of Adam's girlfriends, but they didn't sit around and chat about shit like that.

Nick shrugged, his focus back on the TV again. "Just checking you know what you're doing. His brother's just died, Felix."

"He's missing," Felix corrected without thinking. Jesus. Jamie was rubbing off on him. He snorted as his mind immediately went to the gutter. That earned him a look from both Adam and Nick. "I'm not laughing at that, for fuck's sake. And I know what you're saying, but I don't want to talk about it, okay?"

"Fair enough. I liked him, though, for what it's worth."

Felix smiled. "Good, because he's coming back later."

Adam laughed and shook his head, and Felix could almost hear Nick's eye-roll as he said, "Yeah, absolutely nothing going on there."

"Piss off." He leaned forward and plucked the controller out of Nick's hands. "Now shove over and let me show *you* how it's done." He shouldered Nick out of the way as he slid to the floor. "And tell me what you've been up to since I left."

Felix leaned back against the sofa, concentrated on shooting people on screen, and let Nick and Adam regale him with stories about his old company. It hurt listening to them talk about something he was no longer a part of, but he didn't regret his decision. The timing had been right for him. He'd woken up one morning and felt... done. He'd seen enough, done enough, and that was that.

Chapter Nine

Jamie sat in his car for a good five minutes when he arrived back at the cottage, staring out the windscreen but not registering anything. That kiss… he'd not expected that to happen. He might have thought about Felix in that way — he was a good-looking guy and Jamie wasn't blind — but it had been fleeting, something hiding at the back of his mind. But that kiss had pulled all those feelings kicking and screaming to the forefront, and now it was all Jamie could focus on. He ran a thumb over his bottom lip, still tender from where Felix had run his teeth over it. Jamie shivered and closed his eyes. *Fuck.*

When he opened them and glanced out at the front of the cottage, the stark white building reminded him of why he'd come here in the first place. Guilt crept in, mixing with the lingering arousal, and wasn't that all kinds of messed-up?

He let his head fall back against the seat, and sighed. Never mind Felix kissing him, he should be thinking about everything else that happened that morning. Jamie mulled it over as he sat there, unwilling to go inside yet.

All three of them knew Weston. Felix thought he was involved with the death of his friend, Jason, and Michael's disappearance too. But if he was, then surely the police would have found something when they questioned him? They'd searched the beach and the path up to Weston's house, and even the house itself, and they'd found nothing.

So far as the local police were concerned, Weston had nothing to do with Michael's disappearance. So why was Felix so convinced of his guilt? Jamie remembered the way Felix's voice had broken when he spoke about Jason; maybe Felix's judgment was clouded by what happened to him. Guilt and loss could easily skew a person's view of a situation. All that aside, Michael was still missing, and even though Jamie hated to admit it, with no other explanation available, it was looking more likely that his brother had drowned. For some unfathomable reason, Michael had chosen to walk into the sea, and it had cost him his life.

Jamie sighed and got out of the car, his mood definitely more sombre than when he'd got in it.

The cottage seemed cold and unwelcoming after being inside Felix's. Maybe the absence of other people made it that way, but whatever it was, Jamie was tempted to get in his car and drive back there. Which was ridiculous.

He shook off the feeling and walked into the kitchen to make a drink. The plastic bag full of Michael's belongings sat on the table where Jamie had left it yesterday.

Picking it up from the police station had been bad enough – the officer in charge had been full of sincere condolences. Everyone there thought Michael was dead, and Jamie hadn't missed the pitying looks sent his way as he left with the bag clutched tight to his chest. He'd placed the contents on the kitchen table untouched, too tired and upset to go through them last night. But now curiosity got the better of him, and he slid into one of the chairs and tugged the pile towards him.

He'd told his parents he'd fetched the last of Michael's things, and his mum had wanted to know what was there. Not that knowing would help in any way, but she clung to every little detail Jamie provided. He'd promised to call back later, which was why he now sat staring at the pile of stuff.

Michael's faded uni sweatshirt sat on top, the cuffs frayed and misshapen from where he constantly shoved them up to his elbows. Jamie reached for it and carefully placed it to one side. He remembered Felix saying that day had been hot, so it stood to reason Michael would have taken it off. Underneath it, in another smaller plastic bag, were Michael's watch, wallet, phone, and sunglasses. The wallet still held all his bank cards and thirty pounds in cash. The fact that they were left on the beach further fuelled the police's belief that nobody else had been involved.

Jamie set the small plastic bag on top of the sweatshirt. The final items on the table made his chest hurt. Michael's paints, brushes, and a block of watercolour paper. Jamie flicked through the pages, his breath hitching as he studied the painting inside. Sand clung to the edges, and he took care brushing it off with the tips of his fingers. Even incomplete, the painting was beautiful. His brother had an eye for capturing the sea at its most breathtaking.

The brushes were a little worse for wear, but Jamie didn't bother attempting to clean them. It wasn't as though anyone would be using them again. The thought came more easily that time, and Jamie was forced to accept that maybe everyone else was right, and he was wrong. Either way, his brother was gone, and Jamie was just chasing shadows.

He slumped back in his seat, frowning when his stomach let him know it was way past lunchtime.

Food didn't sound all that appetising, if he was honest, but he made himself a toasted cheese sandwich anyway, more for something to do than anything else. He ate it outside, preferring the open air to the heavy silence of the cottage. Maybe his mum had been right about that too. Staying there didn't seem appealing, all of a sudden.

The sea shimmered under the afternoon sun, and Jamie struggled to look at it without horrible images popping into his head. Christ, he needed something to occupy his mind before he lost it altogether.

A glance at his watch told him it had only been a couple of hours since he'd left Felix's. Was it too soon to go back there? Felix had said any time, but he had his mates there, and despite what Felix had said to the contrary, Jamie felt as though he would be intruding.

The alternative — spending the evening here alone — sounded so miserable that Jamie had his car keys in hand without too much thought. The memory of Felix's mouth on his sent an unexpected jolt of warmth through him and he latched on to that feeling. Maybe it was the last thing he should be thinking about, all things considered, but the idea of doing it again pushed all the other crap to the back of his mind. He needed that.

Grabbing a six-pack of beer from the fridge, Jamie locked the door behind him and headed back to Felix's cottage, hoping Felix really had meant it when he'd said "whenever you like."

The drive back took less time than Jamie expected, and he was pulling up in front of Felix's house in no time. For a split second, he debated whether or not to go in. Maybe this was a mistake… but mistake or not it was better than the alternative. Christ, he never used to be this indecisive. *Get a fucking grip!*

Jamie knocked on the door and waited. Laughter sounded from inside, and then Felix's voice as he shouted something. Jamie couldn't make out any of the words until Felix got closer.

"…That's none of your fucking business." Felix grinned at Jamie as he opened the door. Jamie had the urge to ask "what isn't?", but managed to hold his tongue. Nothing good ever came from eavesdropping, as his mother always said. "Hey." Felix stepped out of the way and motioned for Jamie to go in. "Glad you decided to come back."

Jamie flushed, unable to stop himself glancing at Felix's mouth. His lips were full and inviting, and Jamie's gaze lingered there far too long. "Me too," he answered, finally looking back up.

Instead of laughing or looking smug as Jamie expected, Felix's grin softened into something warmer.

"I brought supplies." Jamie held up the beer and passed it over when Felix reached for it. "Sorry I'm so bloody early. I know you said about eight, but—"

"I believe I said you were welcome back anytime." He ran his tongue over his bottom lip, drawing Jamie's attention again. "Get inside before they come looking for me."

When Jamie brushed past him to go to the living room, Felix stopped him with a hand on his shoulder. "You okay?"

His intense gaze caught Jamie by surprise and made his stomach flutter. Warm breath washed over Jamie's lips. They stood so close that if he leaned in an inch or so, they'd be kissing. "Yeah." Jamie's voice came out low and rough.

The soft "Fuck it" was all the warning he got before Felix backed him up and kissed him.

They touched from chest to midthigh, and Jamie's heart raced from the solid weight of Felix pressing against him. This was so much better than being in the cottage alone.

Shouting from the living room had Felix stepping back again. He gave Jamie a long, lingering look, winked, and then turned towards the noise, trailing a hand across the front of Jamie's jeans.

Jamie hissed and glared at the back of Felix's head as he heard his soft laughter. "Tease," Jamie muttered, resting his head against the wall and closing his eyes for a second. Busy willing the bulge in his jeans to go away, he didn't notice Felix turn back.

Jamie jumped a mile when Felix leaned in to whisper in his ear. "It's only teasing if you don't follow through."

Jamie snapped his eyes open to catch Felix smirking at him, and all his good work was for nothing when he met the dark, heated look in Felix's eyes. He reached down to adjust himself. "Thanks for that." Felix glanced down between them and went to palm Jamie through his jeans, but Jamie shot his hand out, stopping him. "Get lost. I am *not* going in there with a hard-on. In fact, give me those." He grabbed the beer out of Felix's hands and strategically placed it in front of his groin. "I'll join you guys in a sec."

"Sure." Felix gestured down at himself; the outline of his erection was clearly visible against his hip. "But they're going to know." Then he shrugged and headed into the living room before Jamie could stop him.

"Christ." Jamie was rooted to the spot, his cheeks flushed with embarrassment, and he had no idea whether to go wait it out in the kitchen or follow Felix.

"For fuck's sake, Bergie, watch where you point that thing."

"Stop looking at my dick, then."

"Well, don't stand with your groin in my line of sight."

Nick or Adam—Jamie couldn't tell who—made his decision for him. They were going to take the piss regardless; waiting would only delay the inevitable. With an eye-roll and a put-upon sigh, Jamie steeled himself and carried his beer towards the living room.

Three pairs of eyes trained on him, causing him to falter in the doorway. The awkwardness of his earlier exit came back with a jolt and he didn't know whether to bring it up or try to gloss over it.

On the plus side, his hard-on was no longer a problem.

Thankfully, Adam stood quickly and walked over to him, relieving him of his beer. "Finally something decent to drink. You should take note, Felix." He clapped Jamie on the arm, and leaned in close. "Sorry about before. Didn't mean to come off as an insensitive prick."

Jamie nodded, and that was that. Adam handed Jamie one of the beers, told him to take a seat, and then disappeared, presumably to put the rest in the fridge.

Jamie opened his beer and took a drink. Nick nudged him in the shoulder and pointed at Felix with his beer bottle. "Please refrain from feeling him up until we've either gone to bed or passed out. I don't need to see him wandering around at half-mast. It'll put me off my food."

Felix snorted from where he lay sprawled on the floor propped up against the sofa. He reached over and slapped Nick's—very firm, from where Jamie was sitting—belly. "From the looks of it that might not be a bad thing. What the hell have they been feeding you over there?"

Jamie listened to the back-and-forth swapping of insults with amusement, and settled back into the comfy sofa cushions, letting their voices wash over him. It was obvious from the easy way they interacted that they'd known each other years. They must have seen active duty together, and Jamie wondered what sort of bond an experience like that formed between people. He had close friends back home, but nothing like this.

It reminded him sharply of Michael, and he gripped his can of beer tight as the wave of hurt pulled at his chest.

Fuck, I miss him.

"Hey." Felix's hand on his thigh caught Jamie's attention, and he realised with a jolt that they'd stopped talking and all three of them focused on him. "You okay?"

Jamie took a swig of his beer, taking his time to swallow and compose himself. "Yeah, just thinking." Managing a small smile, he hoped that would be the end of it.

Adam and Nick carried on playing *CoD*, but Felix continued to stare at him. "About your brother?"

It was only a question, no pity in his voice, and maybe it was that more than anything that let Jamie relax and smile properly. He loved his brother, and surprisingly enough found he wanted to talk about him. "I miss him." After finishing the rest of his beer, he set it down on the carpet and leaned forward to rest his elbows on his knees. "I know he's not coming back. They'd have found something by now if he was alive. But he was so full of life, I can't imagine him not being around anymore. No matter how much I look at all the evidence, it doesn't seem to sink in."

Felix clapped his hands together and stood, forcing Jamie to look up at him. "I'm going to make a start on dinner. Why don't you come in the kitchen and tell me a bit about him while I cook? Trust me," he added when Jamie frowned, "I think it'll help." Not waiting for Jamie's answer, Felix turned and left the room.

A few seconds passed while Jamie sat there debating whether to follow him or not. What harm could it do? He wanted to talk about Michael, and Felix had offered to listen. Mind made up, he collected his empty can and went after him, leaving Adam and Nick swearing in increasingly creative ways as they tried to kill each other on screen.

He found Felix bent over, searching for something in his cupboards, and Jamie stopped in the doorway to admire the view. Felix was a big guy, tall and considerably built in comparison to Jamie. His jeans hugged his arse, clinging to the firm muscles of his arsecheeks and thighs, making Jamie want to reach out and run his hands over them. Then Felix squatted down to reach into the cupboard, and revealed the black band of his underwear and a strip of smooth, tanned skin.

"Aha! Found it." Felix stood abruptly, holding a large frying pan aloft. Jamie snapped his eyes back up, but not quickly enough. If Felix noticed he didn't call Jamie out on it. He waved the pan at the table and chairs. "Have a seat."

After Felix set the pan on the hob, he fetched them both another beer out of the fridge — the beers Jamie had bought, he noted.

"Thanks." Jamie watched him fetch more things out of the fridge and set them on the counter. "Do you have any brothers or sisters?" he asked, suddenly feeling the urge to know more about Felix.

Felix answered over his shoulder as he unwrapped a pack of minced beef and emptied it into the pan. "Two sisters and a brother. One of my sisters moved up to Scotland last year, the other lives just outside Penzance, and my brother's currently stationed in Afghanistan, due to come home in four weeks."

"Oh." Jamie looked up to see Felix smiling as he worked. "He's in the Army as well?"

"Yep. He got promoted to sergeant last month."

The unmistakeable pride in his voice made Jamie smile. "What made you leave?" he asked, then immediately wished he could take it back when Felix flinched. Clearly it was a sore point and maybe too personal for Jamie to ask when he hardly knew Felix. "Sorry, that's none of my business."

Felix sighed, then stirred the food in the saucepan for long enough that Jamie thought he was ignoring the question. "No, it's fine. It's just—" Felix turned around and leaned against the counter, facing him. "Seeing the guys again makes me really fucking miss it." He scrubbed a hand over his eyes; a wry smile appeared as the noises from the living room got louder and more raucous. And that was only two of them. Jamie couldn't imagine what it must be like in a whole company. "To answer your question, though, I left because it seemed like the right time. I'd done my share of tours, and it didn't hold the same appeal it used to."

"Do you regret it?" Wow, Jamie was asking all the personal questions today. He couldn't seem to help himself.

Felix met his gaze and held it. "No. There are a lot of things I miss about being in the Army, but no. I don't regret leaving." He smiled, and Jamie returned it easily, relieved that he hadn't pissed Felix off with all his prying. "Anything else you want to know? I thought you were going to tell me about your brother."

Jamie flushed and glanced down at his feet. Oh yeah… that was why Felix had invited him into the kitchen. But he was starting to like Felix, and he wanted to know all about him. "I have one more question, then I'm done. I promise."

Felix looked unconvinced, but he nodded. "Go on, then."

"I know you're looking after the cottage and a couple of other properties, but that's temporary, right?" Felix nodded again. "So what are you going to do after that? What does one do when leaving the Army after so many years?"

"So many years?" Felix laughed. "You make me sound ancient."

He looked so much softer around the edges in that moment. And hot too. Jamie glanced down at his mouth, remembering how soft it had felt against his own hours earlier and the scrape of stubble, and he absently rubbed at his lips and chin. "How old are you?" Jamie asked, trying to drag his attention away from Felix's mouth.

"I thought you said one more?"

"I lied, clearly. And you still haven't answered the first one."

Felix half turned back to the hob and stirred the food in the pan, then put the spoon down on the counter. "I'm thirty-two. I joined up when I was eighteen."

"See, I was right with 'all those years.'" Jamie grinned up at him, and when Felix rolled his eyes but smiled at him, he felt lighter than he had in days. "Sorry, carry on."

"I did some courses online in my last year, and I know a few guys who set up their own consulting company when they got out. You know, contracting out to different companies." Jamie nodded. "I asked if they saw many project manager jobs, they said yes and asked if I wanted to join them."

"And you agreed?" Jamie eyed the relaxed way Felix leaned against the kitchen counter. Casual suited him, and Jamie struggled to picture him in a shirt and tie, working in some office. That was one of the perks of working for himself; Jamie didn't miss all the office bullshit one bit.

Felix nodded, though. "I said yes. My first contract starts October 19."

"Oh. That's great, then." Jamie tried to sound sincere, but judging by the way Felix laughed again and shook his head, he'd failed miserably.

"You don't think I'm office material?"

Jamie bit his lip, thinking how to explain without either offending Felix or embarrassing himself. He gestured at Felix's everything. "You're just so... so...." Felix smoothed his hands down his thighs and Jamie's gaze caught and held there.

"So?"

For God's sake! Jamie was good with words—they were his livelihood. How come he couldn't find any now? "So not office material. No."

"Oh? What would you suggest I do?" Felix was definitely amused now, and Jamie grinned back at him, playing along.

It had been a while since he'd flirted with someone like this, and he didn't remember it being this easy and fun. "Something with your hands, maybe. Definitely something outside where you have to take your shirt off a lot." *In for a penny and all that.*

Felix lifted up his T-shirt, revealing his nicely defined six-pack and a thick dark happy trail. "I don't know," he tried to look unsure, but Jamie caught the twitch of his lips as he attempted not to smile. "You think people would want to see this?"

Jamie nodded, his mouth dry all of a sudden. *People would definitely want to see that.* Jamie wanted to lick it. Whatever expression was on his face right then had Felix clearing his throat and dropping his T-shirt.

"I'll keep that in mind." Felix stood up, and Jamie managed to snap his gaze back up to his face. The kitchen felt a lot warmer than it had five minutes ago. "Now you know all about me. It's your turn." He set the pan to simmer and put a lid on it, moving it to the back of the hob.

Jamie shifted in his seat, a little more comfortable. He swallowed to get some moisture back in his mouth after Felix's impromptu flash. "What do you want to know? And what are we having, by the way?"

"Everything. And chilli. It needs to simmer for half an hour or so."

"Nice." Jamie eyed the pan with renewed interest. "And *everything*?" He frowned, wondering where to start. "Okay, but don't blame me if I bore you with details. You did say everything."

Felix shrugged, sipped his beer, and waited.

"I'm thirty years old and I'm self-employed."

"Doing what?"

"Copywriting and media relations." Jamie had no desire to elaborate. Anything he said would be boring as fuck compared to what Felix had been up to for the past fourteen years. "Don't ask me to explain. It'll put us both to sleep."

"But you enjoy what you do?" Felix asked somewhat sceptically.

Jamie did to a certain extent, but work was work. "It has its moments. The best part is I get to work from home most of the time."

Felix glanced out the kitchen window and smiled. "Yeah, I can see the appeal."

"If only my view was like this."

"What about family?" Felix asked softly, clearly aware this part would change the mood instantly.

Jamie's breath caught at the reminder. "My parents and Michael."

"Tell me about them." He smiled encouragingly, and Jamie refused to let himself get upset again. Felix had asked, and there was so much more to his family than an uncertain ending on a beach.

So Jamie talked about his family, telling the funniest stories he could remember about Michael and him growing up. The more he talked, the more he relaxed, and he had to accept that Felix had been right. Talking about his brother's life helped ease the ache in his chest. It didn't go away entirely — not that Jamie expected it ever would — but for this small pocket of time, the relief at being able to laugh and smile was almost overwhelming. He'd forgotten how cathartic laughter could be.

In the middle of telling Felix some story about Michael and his penchant for being naked as a child, Adam and Nick wandered into the kitchen, probably to see what they were up to. A quick glance at the kitchen clock told Jamie they'd been in the kitchen for almost an hour.

"Something smells good." Adam yawned as he came through the door, and stretched his arms up above his head, smiling at the *crack* his back made when he twisted from side to side. It had the added side effect of lifting his T-shirt up a few inches to reveal the smooth planes of a toned, tanned stomach.

Jamie's gaze naturally dropped to Adam's waist without a conscious effort on his part. If a fit guy flashed his belly, then Jamie was going to look. It was like a Pavlovian response. Who wouldn't look? Both Nick and Adam were obviously in great shape and easy on the eye. Dark hair and stubble had always done it for Jamie; add in the bonus of imagining them in uniform and he should be in hog's heaven. But apart from admiring the cut of Adam's abs, his gaze didn't linger.

If he let himself admit it, the ex-soldier leaning against the counter, watching him with a sort of amused frown, had captured his interest days ago. Jamie just hadn't noticed until today.

"What's in the pan?" Adam let his arms drop, seemingly oblivious to Jamie's ogling—thank God—and he wandered over to peer into the large pan on the hob. "Chilli?" He patted his belly when Felix nodded. "I'm fucking starving. When will it be done?"

"About fifteen minutes. I'll put the rice on now." Felix shoved Adam out of the way and fetched another pan out from the cupboard. "Who won?" he glanced between Nick and Adam as he stood there, and Jamie admired the tightness of his jeans again.

Nick's smug smile answered that. "Like you even have to ask."

Felix grinned and gave Adam a consoling pat on the shoulder. "I'm sure you tried your best." The scowl and "Piss off" in return made Jamie think this was a standing joke between them, and he suddenly felt like a spare part. Which, when he stopped to think about it, was probably right.

Except when it was just him and Felix in the kitchen, he hadn't felt anything but relaxed and, for want of a better word, content. Content to forget about everything happening around them and talk for the sake of getting to know him better. No digging for information or ulterior motives. He watched the play of muscles in Felix's back and shoulders as he moved about the kitchen.

Well, maybe one ulterior motive.

Chapter Ten

Felix concentrated on stirring the rice as he felt Nick come to lean against the counter beside him. Nick had a look about him, the irritated one he got when his curiosity got the better of him. He elbowed Felix in the kidney, making him stop and glance up.

"What?" Felix put the spoon down and crossed his arms with a sigh. "Whatever it is, spit it out."

Nick smirked at him, acknowledging how well they knew each other. "Did you see anything interesting when you were spying on Westie?"

Felix cocked an eyebrow. "I thought you said that was a waste of my time?"

"It is, but that doesn't mean I'm not interested in knowing what you saw. If anything."

All three of them stared at him expectantly, and Felix caught Jamie's gaze. He hadn't wanted to get Jamie involved in this part. Weston was a dangerous man, whether he had anything to do with Michael's disappearance or not. But since Felix wasn't going to be watching the house anymore, what could it hurt? If he stopped and considered it rationally, it wasn't as though anything he'd seen could be incriminating evidence.

"Not much, really. You know how I told you that he's been at the house a lot more in the past two weeks?" He paused, looking up and noting Nick's expression. Felix attempted to keep the sarcasm out of his voice as he said, "Probably all the nice weather we've been having."

"Probably." The sudden interest on Nick's face wasn't helpful at all. Felix needed him to be the voice of reason.

"Anyway, a couple of days ago, he had visitors. The first people I've seen going to the house since I've been watching it." Christ, when he said it out loud like that, it sounded ridiculous. What had he been thinking? He was lucky not to have got himself arrested, and how would that have looked on his CV? He shook off the uncomfortable feeling and carried on, eager to get it all out and forget about it. "They didn't stay long, but they came back on Tuesday and it looked like they were staying while Weston left. I haven't been back since, so I don't know for sure. He had a small suitcase with him, so…."

They lapsed into silence, everyone mulling over what he'd just said. Felix pushed away the feeling of stupidity that continued to niggle at him. He wished he'd never fucking said anything in the first place. When he glanced up, Jamie was watching him, his head cocked slightly to the side as though considering something. That couldn't be good. Felix didn't want Jamie having any thoughts concerning Weston.

Adam sighed and walked over to the fridge to get more beer. He handed them out, giving Felix his last. "Let's face it, Weston's probably shady as fuck, but nothing you saw is evidence of a crime. Let it go, and let the police do their job. I'm sure he'll slip up at some point in his life and they'll get him."

Felix picked up the wooden spoon again and started to stir the rice, more for something to do than anything else. "I hope so." He knew Adam was right, but it irritated the fuck out of him when he pictured Weston's arrogant salute the other day at the house.

Adam and Nick seemed happy to drop the subject. They ate dinner at the table, and as predicted, Felix got the piss ripped out of him mercilessly for the next couple of hours. He kept an eye on Jamie, pleased to see him relaxed and happy as he laughed at the blatantly exaggerated stories Adam came out with. No one brought up the subject of Weston or Jason again, but every so often Jamie would catch his eye, and Felix got the distinct impression he wouldn't like what was going on in Jamie's head.

Several hours and several beers later, back in the living room, Nick stood and yawned. "I'm gonna call it a night." He kicked Felix where he sat sprawled on the floor leaning against the sofa next to Jamie. They'd sat like that for ages, touching from thigh to shoulder. "I promised Claire I'd be home by lunchtime," Nick carried on. "I don't want to feel like shit in the morning."

Adam sat on the other sofa with his head resting against the back. He glanced sleepily at Nick and then down to Felix and Jamie. A lazy grin appeared. "I think I'll come with you." He stood too, scratching at his belly. "Leave these two lovebirds to it."

Felix groaned and covered his face with his hands. "Fuck off and go to bed already," he muttered through his fingers. He didn't give a shit what they said, but Jamie had tensed immediately. "The beds are all made up, decide between you who takes the blow up one. I'll see you tossers in the morning for breakfast."

"You going to cook it?" Adam asked, stepping over Felix's legs on his way out.

"Of course."

"Can't wait." Adam glanced at Jamie and winked. "Night."

Felix rolled his eyes. *Knob.*

Adam stopped behind Nick at the door. "I'd offer you my bed, Jamie, but I don't think you're going to need it." He laughed as Felix glared daggers at him, and he and Nick disappeared from view.

Felix listened to them stomp up the stairs like a herd of elephants, fully expecting plaster dust to rain down on him. "Christ, they're heavy-footed bastards."

Jamie nodded silently. He drew his knees up and rested his arms on them, not looking at Felix. "Just the one spare room, then?"

"Yep." Felix turned his head a touch to watch Jamie out of the corner of his eye. He still faced forward, hands clasped loosely together. "And this sofa."

Jamie nodded but offered no comment. Felix wondered what was going through his head. He hadn't made a move on Jamie with his mates there, for obvious reasons. Adam had been less than subtle with his exit, though, and now a tension filled the space around them that hadn't been there before. Felix hated it. This was his home, for now. He shouldn't feel on edge.

Fuck it! No sense beating about the bush, they were both adults.

Felix grabbed the remote, turned the TV off, and shifted to face Jamie. He said, "Do you want to come upstairs with me?" at the same time as Jamie whispered, "I want you to take me to Weston's house."

Felix stared at him. Obviously they weren't on the same page at all. "What?"

Jamie's cheeks were tinged pink, whether from Felix's question or the way Felix was now glaring at him in disbelief.

"You want to do what exactly?"

Sitting up and crossing his legs, Jamie looked up at Felix. He had a determined set to his shoulders and a challenge in his blue eyes. "I want you to take me to the place you watched Weston's house from. I want to see him for myself."

Felix knew Jamie had been thinking about something like this. Damn it, why had Nick insisted on bringing it up so bloody much? "No. Not a fucking chance."

Jamie narrowed his eyes. "Why not?"

"Because for one, it's probably classed as stalking. Two" — he counted them off on his fingers — "he's a dangerous man. And three, there's no fucking point. You heard what Nick said earlier, and he was right. You're not going to see anything, and it won't give you any of the answers you're looking for."

"You've been going there every day since I got here," Jamie forged on undeterred. "What's one more bloody time?"

"No." Felix sat up straight. He wanted to grasp Jamie by the shoulders and shake him. Sometimes all it took was "one more bloody time." He'd been an idiot to keep going up there, obsessed with the idea of proving Weston's guilt, and not seeing how stupid it all was. But most of all, he'd been lucky. Lucky that nothing had happened and no one had reported him. No way was he risking another trip there.

Felix grabbed one of Jamie's hands, where he'd curled them into fists on the carpet, and prised his fingers open. "What good will it do to go up there just to watch his house?" He wrapped his hand around Jamie's and smoothed a thumb over his knuckles. "Let it go."

As soon as the words were out of his mouth, Felix knew he'd said the wrong thing.

Jamie snatched his hand back and scrambled to his feet. "*Let it go?*" he hissed, glaring down at Felix. "That's my fucking brother we're talking about." He narrowed his eyes and pointed at Felix. "You can't *let it go*, and your friend died months ago, so don't fucking lecture me." He turned and stalked over to the window, looking out into the darkness.

Felix clenched his fists at the mention of Jason, but refused to be drawn into an argument. They were both a little drunk, and Jamie was upset. He wasn't going to make it worse if he could help it. "I was wrong."

Jamie sighed and rested his ahead against the glass. When he spoke again, Felix had to strain to hear him. "It's easy for you. You know Jason's dead. At least there was a body for you to bury and mourn. We've got *nothing*." His shoulders sagged in defeat.

Felix knew Jamie hadn't meant to be so flippant, but he couldn't sit there and listen to him saying Felix had it *easy*. "Hey!" He shot up off the floor and pulled Jamie's arm to turn him around and shove him against the patio door. "I know you're going through a shit time right now, but that doesn't give you the right to tell me how fucking *easy* Jason's death was for me." Anger bubbled up inside him, and he struggled to rein it back. "Jason had no family. His parents died when we were out in Iraq, so I was his emergency contact. It was me they called first when he died. I had to go and see the fucking body to identify him. Do you have any idea what that's like?"

Jamie shook his head, his eyes wide as he stared back at Felix. "No," he whispered, his voice raw with emotion.

"No, I didn't think so." Felix let go of Jamie's arm, not missing the way Jamie rubbed at where Felix's fingers had left angry red marks. Shit, he needed to get a hold of himself. "Fuck, sorry." He reached out and put his hand over Jamie's. "The last time me and Jason talked, we argued, and I never got a chance to say sorry. I can't even remember him like he used to be because when I try, all I see is him cold and lifeless and laid out on a fucking slab." Closing his eyes, Felix concentrated on breathing in and out and the feel of Jamie's skin under his fingertips. "So please don't try and tell me that any of it is easy."

Silence filled the room. Felix's heart pounded loud in his ears, the rush of adrenaline taking its time to drain away. A firm hand on his jaw was followed by a whispered "I'm sorry."

When Felix opened his eyes, Jamie had moved closer, close enough for Felix to slip an arm around his waist. He gripped onto the material of Jamie's T-shirt, wondering what Jamie would do next.

Jamie had a determined glint in his eyes, and for once Felix wanted someone else to decide the next move. He felt adrift, like he had after Jason's death, and he met Jamie's gaze, willing him to do something, anything to anchor Felix in place.

"I shouldn't have said that." Jamie cupped Felix's face and drew him in for a soft kiss, the barest brush of lips. It set Felix's whole body alight. "I know it wasn't easy. It'll never be easy." Stepping closer, Jamie kissed him again, aligning their bodies so Felix felt Jamie's warmth seep into him everywhere they touched.

Felix sagged against him, relief coursing through his veins because *this…* this was exactly what he needed. His back hit the wall as Jamie manoeuvred them; the cool brick was a sharp contrast to Jamie's heat pressed along his front. Felix shivered, wanting to sink into Jamie and lose himself for a while.

He had a couple of inches on Jamie and definitely more muscle, but it was Jamie who had him pinned against the wall then, Jamie who took control and tilted Felix's head to deepen the kiss, and Jamie who shoved his thigh between Felix's legs to rub against his groin. It was hot as fuck, and Felix ached with how hard it made him.

Felix groaned as Jamie thrust up, his thigh pressing into Felix's erection and his cock nudging against Felix's hip, more than happy to let Jamie manhandle him. But he didn't want to come in his jeans, and the prospect was getting more likely with Jamie grinding against him like that and kissing down the side of his neck. "Hey." It sounded more like a breathy moan than a word, and Jamie hummed against his throat in response. With great effort on his part, Felix put his hands on Jamie's chest and pushed him away enough to meet his gaze. "Let's go to bed." He felt a little smug at how long it took Jamie to focus and answer him.

"What about the others?"

Felix raised an eyebrow. "I'm not sure they'll be up for a foursome, they're probably asleep by now."

Jamie's resulting smile made Felix's stomach flutter. He laughed and said, "As tempting as that is, I meant won't they hear us?"

Felix grinned back. "Are you planning on being loud?"

From the way Jamie immediately flushed, Felix thought not. But then he leaned closer to whisper in Felix's ear. "That depends on you, doesn't it?"

Felix reached down to adjust himself as his dick throbbed, caught at an awkward angle in his jeans. "Christ," he muttered, pushing Jamie back and grabbing his hand. "It's an old cottage and the walls are thick." He tugged Jamie towards the stairs. "And at this point, I don't give a shit if they hear us. They've heard worse, believe me."

Jamie looked as though he wanted to ask about that, but Felix didn't give him the chance. He started up the steps pulling Jamie behind him.

"I'm coming. Jesus." Jamie's soft laughter sounded behind him.

Felix slowed his pace, looking back over his shoulder with a smirk. "They probably heard that." Jamie squeezed Felix's hand hard in retaliation, so Felix winked and said none too quietly, "*Ow*, not so hard."

The expression on Jamie's face was priceless. Felix tripped up the stairs, he was laughing so much. The door to the spare room stayed shut as they passed it, thank God. Felix wouldn't have put it past one of them to come out and take the piss.

Finally they tumbled through the second door along the corridor and into Felix's bedroom. Felix shut and locked it behind them. He'd left the bedside lamp on earlier, and the soft glow bathed the room in a warm low light. Leaning back against the door frame, he watched Jamie stand and take stock of his bedroom. His mum and dad had helped decorate the place when it was finished, and now that Felix thought about it, this room looked a lot like the one they had at home.

The curtains and bedding were white with red, yellow, and orange flowers, and the numerous cushions adorning the bed were all in matching colours. Personally he didn't care what was on his sheets; the bed was comfy, and that was enough.

Obviously the decor tickled Jamie because he glanced back at Felix, not bothering to hide his grin. "It doesn't exactly scream manly ex-soldier, does it?"

Felix shrugged and kept a straight face. "The handcuffs and paddles are under the bed."

The uncertain look on Jamie's face was too much, and Felix couldn't stop from smiling at him. "Your face."

Jamie walked over and stood in front of him. "Funny."

"I thought so." He hooked his fingers in Jamie's belt loops and pulled him closer. "Now where were we?"

"I believe—" Jamie slid a hand down to cup Felix through his jeans, making him groan. "—you wanted to get these off." He began to undo Felix's belt, pulling it undone at a snail's pace and batting

Felix's hands out of the way when he went to do it quicker. "What's the rush?"

Felix grabbed Jamie's hand, put it back on his cock, and pressed down. His boxers were damp, and he wondered if Jamie could feel it through the denim. "This isn't going to wait long." He bit his lip, enjoying Jamie's firm touch a little too much. "Come on." He reached for the hem of Jamie's T-shirt and drew it up and off, tossing it on the floor next to them.

Slightly paler than Felix, Jamie's tanned skin glowed in the muted light of the bedroom. A dusting of blond hair covered his chest, and a thin line of it led below the waistband of his jeans. Felix licked his lips as he laid a hand on the flat of Jamie's stomach. The skin felt warm under his fingertips, and he dragged his hand up over Jamie's chest, letting his thumb graze over a nipple.

Jamie sucked in a breath, and Felix glanced up to find blue eyes watching him intently. "Okay?" Felix whispered, rubbing his thumb slowly back and forth.

Jamie nodded, swallowing thickly, and Felix bent to lick along the jut of his collarbone.

"Yours too." Jamie's voice came out husky as he tugged on the bottom of Felix's T-shirt. "Take it off." He helped push it up over Felix's head, and let it drop to the floor. Then Jamie's hands were on Felix's chest, one sliding up to wrap around the back of his neck and pull him into a kiss, the other splayed across the taut muscles of his abdomen. "Fuck," Jamie muttered. His grip on Felix was rough and demanding, and Felix let himself be turned and backed up towards the edge of the bed. When it nudged up against the back of his knees, Jamie stopped and took a small step back.

Felix noted with some satisfaction the way Jamie's jeans strained at the front, and he reached out to run his thumb up along the taut denim. Jamie's breathing, already a little ragged, stuttered, and he gasped softly as Felix rubbed at the head of his cock before going for his belt buckle.

He glanced up to see Jamie watching him intently with his lip pulled between his teeth. "Yeah?" They seemed to be of the same mind, but Felix wanted to be absolutely sure.

Jamie ran his tongue over his lip where his teeth had been, and smiled. "God, yeah."

For a second or two, neither of them moved, Felix couldn't look away from Jamie's heated gaze until his hands joined Felix's on his belt buckle, and then they were struggling to undo belts and buttons and zips in a flurry of movement that had them both collapsing on the bed, breathless.

And naked.

Jamie lay on his back, lean and glorious. Dark blond hair covered his legs, and Felix moved onto his side to drag a hand appreciatively up the length of Jamie's thigh, loving the coarse prickle of hairs under his palm.

"What do you want?" Jamie took hold of his cock and started to stroke himself in a slow steady rhythm. Felix felt hypnotized, unable to look away as he watched Jamie's fist close over the head and then slide back down again and again. "Or are you just going to watch?"

The amused tone caught Felix's attention, and he wrapped his hand around Jamie's, matching his movements. "Not this time, no."

In the heat of the moment, Felix couldn't imagine there not being a next time. Jamie felt so good under his hands. He wanted to touch him everywhere, feel him everywhere, but despite his best intentions, that wasn't going to happen now. His own neglected cock brushed against Jamie's hip, and he shifted into a better position, leaving a trail of sticky wetness on his skin.

"Well?" Seemingly impatient for Felix's answer, Jamie pushed up into their combined grip, and under the circumstances, he fixed Felix with an impressive glare. "Never figured you for the indecisive type."

Before Felix could reply, Jamie gripped Felix's dick in his free hand and grinned. "I'd really like you to fuck me with this." The gravelly sound to Jamie's voice sent a shudder of anticipation down Felix's spine and he cursed under his breath as Jamie tightened his grip. "How does that sound?"

Fucking awesome. But if Jamie didn't stop touching him like that, they were never going to get that far. He grabbed Jamie's wrists, and in a move that turned out smoother than he expected, rolled on top of Jamie and pushed his hands up onto the pillows above his head. "Sounds good to me."

He leaned in to capture Jamie's mouth in what was meant to be a quick kiss before reaching for supplies, but Jamie spread his legs wider, hooked an ankle over Felix's thigh, and kissed him back hard.

Helpless to do anything but go with it, Felix pushed his hips forward and moaned as his cock rubbed against Jamie's. It felt too good not to do it a couple more times, so Felix rolled his hips and kissed Jamie until he was almost dizzy with lack of air and they broke apart, both breathing heavily.

Jamie flexed his fingers and Felix immediately let go of his wrists.

"Sorry." Felix rubbed gently at the slight redness on Jamie's skin, but Jamie shook his head.

"Don't be. I like it." Now that his hands were free, he wasted no time grabbing hold of Felix's arsecheeks and thrusting up against him. Felix was still processing his words and wondering what else he might like, and the sudden move took him by surprise. He arched into it, but Jamie stopped him with a squeeze and a breathy laugh. "Fuck, stop, or I'm gonna come." After letting go of Felix's arse, Jamie pushed at his shoulder until Felix acquiesced and rolled onto his back. "Condoms, lube?" Jamie grinned down at him as he straddled his lap.

"Top drawer." Felix nodded at the bedside table next to them, and put his hands on Jamie's waist to steady him as he reached over.

A condom and the half-empty bottle of lube landed on the bed next to Felix's shoulder, and Jamie settled back in position on Felix's thighs. He reached for the condom with one hand and Felix's cock with the other. "I'll do this part." Felix gritted his teeth as Jamie rolled the condom down at a teasingly slow pace, and reached for the lube. He passed it to Felix with a sly grin. "You can do this bit."

Slicking his fingers and then coaxing Jamie up a little so that he could reach, Felix opened him up with as much patience as he could manage, while trying to ignore the hand on his dick.

The third time he rubbed against Jamie's prostate, Jamie swore and pushed on Felix's arm to get him to stop. "That's enough." He flashed Felix a small smile, then rose up on his knees.

Felix put a hand on Jamie's hip to steady him and then shuffled to line up his cock. Holding his breath, Felix stayed as still as possible while Jamie eased himself down, his fingers digging into Felix's arms hard enough to hurt if Felix could have felt anything but the tight heat of Jamie's body.

With Felix buried deep inside him, Jamie let his head drop and took a shuddering breath.

"Okay?" It came out as barely a whisper, but Felix couldn't manage anything more. He massaged Jamie's hips, his thighs, and anywhere else he could reach, and waited for Jamie to say something, or move, or do anything to show he was all right. "Jamie?" It was the first time Felix had used his name since they'd come up here, and it felt strangely intimate on his tongue.

"I'm good." Jamie's voice was tight and strained, but the soft huff of laughter that followed eased Felix's nerves. "Just give me a minute. It's been a while, and you're not exactly small."

"You can still talk, so I can't be all—"

Jamie gave an experimental roll of his hips, and it cut Felix off and made him moan. "Shut up and fuck me."

Felix had years of experience at taking orders from people above him, and he wasn't about to refuse now. He grinned up at Jamie and whispered, "Yes, sir."

Jamie's answering laughter died in his throat as Felix held him tight and thrust up as best he could manage from flat on the bed. He couldn't get much leverage, but then Jamie leaned forward, allowing Felix to bring his knees up, and between them they got a rhythm going.

Jamie sank down as Felix pushed up, and the soft sounds of skin on skin filled the room. Sweat trickled down Felix's temples and clung to the back of his neck as he struggled to hold back his orgasm and make Jamie come first.

Heat filled Felix's belly, wrapping around him as pleasure built inside. A quick glance up at Jamie's face had Felix desperate with the need to let go. Jamie had his eyes shut tight, his head back, and his mouth slightly open, and Felix wanted to kiss him so badly. "Come here." He lifted up and tugged Jamie down at the same time, resulting in a messy kiss that was more heavy breathing than anything else. But it was enough. "Fuck, Jamie...."

Unable to stop it, Felix held Jamie firmly in place and thrust up one more time. He emptied in one shuddering pulse after another, vaguely aware of Jamie swearing in his ear as he fisted his cock and came all over Felix's chest.

Jamie slumped forward, bracing himself on his elbows, and he dropped his head onto Felix's shoulder. "God, I needed that."

Felix would concur if he could be bothered to speak. Instead he closed his eyes and patted Jamie on the back, making him shake with silent laughter. It had the unfortunate effect of making Felix's cock slide out a little and forcing him into action. With a groan he gripped the bottom of the condom and gently urged Jamie to get off him.

Post-orgasm, Felix's limbs were heavy and clumsy, and it took all his effort to get up and dispose of it in the bathroom bin. Thank God his aunt had installed an en-suite. It might be tiny with only a sink and a toilet in it, but it saved him the hassle of leaving the room and possibly meeting someone out on the landing. Wetting a flannel, he half-heartedly wiped at his chest and stomach before rinsing it and taking it to Jamie.

Felix stopped in the bathroom doorway to admire the sight of Jamie sprawled out over his bed with his eyes closed. He was lying flat on his back, legs spread, with one arm above his head. His blond hair was stuck to his forehead with sweat, his lips were red and a little swollen, and his cock rested against his belly, still thick but not fully hard anymore. He looked thoroughly fucked.

The thought sent a ripple of heat to Felix's groin—not that he'd be up for round two anytime soon. The combination of alcohol and sex had exhausted him, and he wanted nothing more than to curl up next to Jamie and sleep. Flannel in hand, he walked over to the bed and sat down on the side nearest Jamie. "Hey." He nudged Jamie's hip until Jamie opened one eye and blinked a couple of times, focusing on Felix. "Want me to?"

"Hmm?" Jamie pushed himself up on one elbow, glanced at the cloth in Felix's hand, then shook his head and reached out to take it from him. When he was done, he handed it back and collapsed on the bed.

Felix got up and walked over to toss the cloth into the bathroom, closing the door after. When he turned back, Jamie was awake and watching him.

"Want me to sleep on the couch?"

Felix stopped in his tracks and stared back at him. It hadn't occurred to him to ask Jamie to leave, and now Jamie had brought it up, he wondered if it should have. What were they doing, exactly? A quick fuck to relieve tension, or what? Felix had no clue, and he was way too tired to attempt to read what was going on in Jamie's head. As he usually did in these situations, he went with his gut instinct.

"No." He walked over to the other side of the bed and climbed in. "What I want is for you to get under this quilt and go to sleep." He smiled, and Jamie grinned back at him.

"Okay, then."

Felix fell asleep with his arm draped over Jamie's waist and his nose pressed to the back of his neck. His instinct had never steered him wrong yet.

Chapter Eleven

Jamie woke with a start, his heart racing, and it took a good few seconds to realise he'd been dreaming and whatever had been chasing him wasn't real.

"Shit." He rubbed the sleep from his eyes and then promptly froze when a warm, strong arm slipped around his waist and drew him back against an even warmer body.

The previous night came back to him in a rush of vivid images and feelings. He flushed as he remembered Felix's hands on him. Heat pooled in his belly, encouraging his morning wood to full hardness. Felix muttered something in his sleep, then burrowed his nose into the crook of Jamie's neck with a sigh. The act seemed so at odds with Felix's tough-guy exterior it made Jamie grin and relax back into his embrace.

It might get awkward when he woke up, but Jamie got the feeling it wouldn't. Felix didn't seem like the sort to beat around the bush. Whatever that had been last night, Jamie fully expected him to spell it out in no uncertain terms. And he'd already invited Jamie to his house when he had guests, so Jamie couldn't see him kicking him out just because they'd had sex—really hot, wouldn't-mind-a-repeat-performance sex.

Reaching down to lazily palm his cock, Jamie wondered if it would be rude to wake Felix up now. He was all set and ready to go; it would be a shame to waste it. He shuffled back enough to press flush against Felix's front and grinned when he felt an answering firmness against his arse. Felix moaned and tightened his grip on Jamie. Felix's fingers splayed out on Jamie's stomach, then stilled, and Jamie's smile widened as Felix woke up and realised where he was and who he was wrapped around.

"Hey." His voice was morning rough and so sexy. Slowly, Felix slid his hand farther down until it met Jamie's cock, now straining up towards his belly. "You're up early."

Jamie laughed and pushed up into the loose grip Felix had on him. "So it would seem."

"It'd be a shame to waste it." He rubbed his dick against Jamie's arse and kissed the back of his neck.

"Hmm… my thoughts exactly."

With the slow, lazy grind of Felix behind him and the tight grip of Felix's hand on his cock, Jamie closed his eyes and let himself be taken care of. Soft grunts and the rustle of sheets as they moved beneath them were all the sounds they made. Lost in the feel of Felix all around him, Jamie imagined waking up to this every morning. Having someone touch him like this made it hard not to want more of it.

He came with a soft moan, bucking up into Felix's hand and spilling over his belly and the sheet underneath them. Felix followed soon after, pressed up against Jamie's back.

Sticky wetness trickled over Jamie's skin, and he groaned into the pillow. "I need a shower."

"Yeah, you're all dirty."

The smile in Felix's voice was hard to miss, and then rough fingertips ran through the mess on Jamie's back. He rolled his eyes, but there was no denying the small thrill that ran through him when Felix did it.

"There isn't a shower in the en-suite, but you can use the one in the main bathroom if you want. I'd hurry, though. Those two are early risers, and I doubt you want to meet them on the landing like this, do you?" He gave Jamie's arse a squeeze with sticky fingers.

"God, no. And stop making it worse. I'm filthy enough as it is."

Felix grinned against the back of Jamie's neck. "Is there such a thing?"

Jamie ignored him in favour of getting up and heading to the shower before Nick or Adam caught him covered in come. Jamie paused in the middle of the bedroom, not wanting to put his clothes on, dirty as he was, but not wanting to go out there naked. Glancing back at Felix, still sprawled out in bed under the quilt, he gestured to his naked form. "A little help?"

Felix put his hands behind his head and grinned. "I don't know… I quite like you like that."

"I doubt Nick and Adam would feel the same."

Felix grimaced. "There should be towels in the en-suite. Use one of them."

"Thanks."

With all the important stuff covered but still hoping he made it to the bathroom without meeting either man, Jamie hurried out of the room for a quick shower.

Wearing the same clothes as the day before, but clean at least, Jamie walked down the stairs towards the smell of bacon and the sound of laughter. He paused in the kitchen doorway, suddenly feeling the awkwardness that hadn't been there earlier.

"Morning."

Three pairs of eyes glanced back at him.

"Morning," Nick and Adam answered at the same time.

Jamie nodded distractedly, his focus taken wholly by the sight of Felix standing half naked by the cooker. His pyjama pants barely clung to his hips, giving the impression they might slip at any moment. Realising he was staring at Felix's arse, Jamie dragged his gaze up over the smooth planes of Felix's back and shoulders. All that taut muscle on display left his mouth uncomfortably dry.

"Hey." Felix turned and smiled at him, his eyes full of mischief, and Jamie blushed before he even said anything else. "You hungry?" Felix gestured to the bacon and eggs he was dishing out.

Jamie had to clear his throat twice before words would come out. "Yeah, thanks." He noted with relief that Felix also leaned over to flick the kettle on.

"There's juice on the table too." Felix gestured with his wooden spoon, and although Jamie hesitated to sit opposite Adam and Nick—who knew what they'd heard last night?—his thirst won out.

He sat and reached for one of the glasses on the table, avoiding looking at either of them for as long as possible. When enough time had passed that it was either acknowledge them or appear rude, Jamie finally looked up. And was met with matching shit-eating grins. *Oh God.*

"You know…," Adam began, pushing the jug of orange juice across the table to Jamie.

"Thanks," Jamie muttered, already cringing.

"...I always thought the rooms in these old cottages were virtually soundproof since they built them with thick walls." Adam's smile got even bigger and Nick nodded, also grinning, next to him.

"The walls are pretty thick," Nick joined in, sounding almost serious. "But you have to account for the doors. The ones upstairs are old, and they don't fit snug to the frame anymore."

"Ah, so that's why you can hear what's going on in the rest of the cottage?"

"Yep."

"With startling and slightly disturbing clarity."

"Yep."

Jamie had his head bent and his eyes closed by this point; his face was flaming, and he fervently wished he'd snuck out the front door instead of coming into the kitchen. *What the fuck was I thinking?* He glanced up as Felix slammed two plates down in front of Nick and Adam.

"Leave him alone, for fuck's sake." Felix put a hand on Jamie's shoulder and gave it a squeeze. "Ignore these two dickheads. They forget that not everyone appreciates their less-than-subtle humour."

Jamie flushed with unexpected warmth at Felix's protectiveness. Of course that all fled with his next sentence. With a smug smile firmly in place, Felix stood, his hand still on Jamie's shoulder.

"They're just pissed that I got some last night and they didn't." He walked past and roughly tousled Adam's hair. "Nick refuse to put out again?"

Adam laughed as he picked up his knife and fork and started to eat. Nick gave Felix the middle-finger treatment. "I'll make sure to tell Claire you suggested I cheat on her."

"You do that. Tell her it was with Adam, and I bet she'd want to watch."

Nick shrugged and grinned. "Yeah, you're probably right." He reached for the brown sauce, and that, apparently, was that.

Army guys are weird.

Felix sat down next to Jamie and nudged his knee under the table. When Jamie looked up at him, Felix winked and then smiled. "Eat your breakfast before it gets cold."

Jamie hadn't even noticed Felix putting a plate in front of him, but there it was. "Thanks."

Felix nodded, and the room lapsed into silence as they ate.

Much to Jamie's surprise, Nick and Adam were packed and ready to go by ten o'clock. Apparently they had plans they'd put off for a day to come and see Felix. They both shook Jamie's hand, and Adam gave him a friendly — if a little harder than Jamie expected — clap on the shoulder and then Jamie hung back by the front door as Felix walked over to their car with them.

They were far enough away or talking quietly enough that Jamie couldn't make out what they were saying. Since they were usually loud, he figured it must have been about him, which was embarrassing. Whatever it was had Felix rolling his eyes and shaking his head. Jamie shifted uncomfortably where he leaned against the doorjamb, and wondered for about the tenth time that morning why he hadn't got up and driven home while everyone was in bed.

Because you like him, his mind helpfully supplied.

Jamie waved when they finally drove away, and he watched Felix turn and saunter over to him, positive he wasn't imagining the predatory way Felix eyed him up. Felix licked his lips. It sent a shiver of heat through Jamie, and just like that, staying was definitely the best decision he'd made that morning.

"So." Felix stopped in front of him, close enough for Jamie to slide his arms around Felix's waist, splaying his hands wide to feel all that warm bare skin, and then resting them on Felix's lower back.

"So?"

Felix's gaze was too intent, too serious, and Jamie ducked his head, choosing to nuzzle along Felix's neck and shoulder instead. Faint traces of shower gel and aftershave clung to Felix's skin, along with the heady smell of sweat and sex. Jamie took a deep breath, letting the reminder of what they'd done fill his lungs.

Felix groaned and pushed him up against the door frame, his larger body caging Jamie in and pressing him into the wood behind. Not the most comfortable of positions, but Jamie hardly noticed; the swell of Felix's dick against his belly took most of his focus. He shifted his hips, and they both gasped at the friction. Jamie wanted nothing more than to go back upstairs and have a repeat performance, but somewhere in the back of his mind, he knew he had plans for today. Plans that weren't staying in bed all day fucking Felix.

As his mind finally focused on what he'd been meaning to do later, reality flooded back with a cold hard slap of guilt.

He needed to pack the rest of Michael's things. *Jesus Christ*, how could he stand there thinking about sex when his brother was still missing?

Sensing the sudden change, Felix let go of him and took a step back. "Everything okay?"

Jamie ran a hand through his hair and shook his head. "What are we even doing?"

"What do you mean?"

"I came down here to collect my missing brother's belongings and maybe get some answers." He gestured wildly between the two of them. "Not for… not… whatever this is."

"Hey." Felix put his hands on Jamie's shoulders, holding him steady. "Calm down."

Jamie shook off Felix's hands and shoved past him onto the gravel drive. "Don't tell me to calm down." He took a couple of steps and then stopped, fully aware how irrational he was being, but unable to stop himself. His mood had shifted so suddenly it left him reeling. "I don't know what to do anymore." Blowing out a harsh breath, he looked up at the sky and attempted to calm his racing heart.

The deep blue, marred here and there by the off-white clouds, was such a contrast to the mixed feelings swirling inside him. He was still half-hard, for fuck's sake. One minute he'd been seconds away from dragging Felix back upstairs, and the next he felt like the worst brother ever. Here he was shacking up with someone he'd known less than a week, while his brother — or his brother's body — was still out there somewhere.

The crunch of gravel behind him had Jamie spinning around to face Felix. "What the hell is wrong with me?"

Felix frowned but didn't stop until he was close enough to take Jamie's face in both his hands, ignoring his protests. He smoothed the pads of his thumbs across Jamie's cheekbones and rested their foreheads together. "Just because we had sex doesn't automatically make you a shit brother. The last two weeks must have been incredibly draining for you. I can't imagine how you feel right now, but you can't spend every minute of every day punishing yourself for something that wasn't your fault."

Jamie opened his mouth to protest, and Felix shushed him with a quick but firm kiss.

"I wasn't finished." He waited until Jamie nodded before carrying on. "Yesterday was intense. The things we talked about brought up some rough memories for me, and I'm sure it wasn't easy for you either. I needed last night. I wanted to lose myself in something physical and easy and really fucking good." He grinned, and Jamie couldn't stop himself smiling back. Felix's smile was infectious. "Did I think beyond getting you naked and in my bed? No. But does that have to be a bad thing?"

Jamie shook his head; the tight feeling in his chest had eased at Felix's words. "What now, though?" In the harsh light of day, "fuck it, let's have sex because I've had a shit day" didn't seem quite so simple as it had last night.

"Is there anything that you absolutely have to do today? Anything that can't wait?"

Jamie bit his lip. "I was going to pack up the rest of Michael's things."

When he said it out loud like that, he realised it was the last thing he felt like doing. That would be it, then. It felt so final, and his heart hurt just thinking about it. It must have shown on his face because Felix kissed him again, slow and soft, soothing the ache in Jamie's chest with each brush of his lips.

Wanting to feel the same sense of escape he'd felt last night, Jamie wrapped his arms around Felix and let his strength ground him. When they finally pulled apart, the jumble of emotions inside him had calmed, and he sighed in relief.

Felix smiled. "Spend the weekend with me."

"But—"

"Michael's things will still be there in a day or two, and you have your phone, so people can contact you if they need to. Please stay."

Jamie thought about it. The sun shone down, warming his back, and if he was honest, going back to the rental cottage held no appeal whatsoever. He wanted to stay with Felix, but he couldn't shake the feeling that he shouldn't be enjoying himself under such dire circumstances. He had less than a week left at the cottage before he needed to get back. If he didn't take this opportunity, there probably wouldn't be another. Was he ready to give up Felix just yet? Michael had always told him to go with his instincts and to stop overthinking things. He'd never listened before; maybe this time he should.

Felix pulled him in for a hug as though reading his thoughts, and all of a sudden, the answer was simple. "Yes. I'll stay."

Chapter Twelve

"Thank fuck." Felix closed his eyes and smiled against Jamie's neck. Whether justified or not, Felix got the impression if Jamie had said no and left, that would have been the last time Felix saw him. And he wanted to keep Jamie to himself for a little bit longer.

Despite all the egging on from Nick and Adam, who apparently thought, "He's the best thing to happen to you in a long while, Felix. Maybe keep this one," he wasn't naive enough to think they were going to fall in love and live happily ever after. Jamie lived in Nottingham, and Felix had a job waiting for him in Reading. And they hardly knew each other. The sex was hot, though, and what could it hurt to have a little fun for a couple of days? God knew they could both do with the distraction.

Taking Jamie's hand in his, Felix led him back inside and upstairs to his bedroom. The cottage was eerily quiet with the absence of his friends. Felix stopped at the doorway of his room and turned to face Jamie. He hooked his finger in the waistband of Jamie's jeans and coaxed him closer. "Now that they're gone, we can be as loud as you like." He smiled, remembering how noisy Jamie had been regardless of Adam and Nick down the hall. "Not that you seemed remotely bothered last night."

He expected Jamie to blush and wasn't disappointed, but Jamie also smiled and winked at him.

"I can be a lot louder."

Jamie palmed Felix's dick through his pyjamas, rubbing his fingers over the hardening length until

Felix grabbed his hand and stilled it. Walking backwards towards his bed, he tugged Jamie after him, not stopping until the pair of them sprawled on top of the quilt. "Show me."

They stayed in bed for the next few hours. Felix couldn't remember the last time he'd spent the morning having sex with someone. He stretched his arms above his head, the pull on his muscles relieving the ache that set in after gripping onto Jamie so hard. He yawned and turned on his side, smiling at the sight of Jamie still very much asleep.

They'd dozed off after mutual blowjobs, but Felix hadn't been able to stay asleep, too used to getting up early and keeping busy. He hated inactivity, and as nice as it was to laze around watching Jamie sleep, he also itched to get up and do things.

The quilt barely covered the top of Jamie's arse, and Felix gave him an appreciative once-over. Jamie had broad shoulders, but he was a lot leaner than Felix. The smooth expanse of his back tapered down to narrow hips and the gentle swell of his arse. The whole thing was far too tempting, and Felix reached out and slowly traced a finger down Jamie's spine.

The soft touch of Felix's fingertip had Jamie moaning into his pillow. Felix smiled as Jamie arched into Felix's hand like a needy cat, only turning to face him when Felix stopped.

"Carry on. S'nice." Jamie opened one eye and looked at him.

Felix grinned but resumed his stroking, rolling his eyes at Jamie's content sigh. Felix's earlier eagerness to get up faded somewhat. Touching Jamie like this was soothing for him too, and he lost himself in the repetitive motion of it, wondering how the events of the last week had led them to end up here. Lying in bed with Jamie was far more relaxed and comfortable than it had any right to be.

The silence stretched long enough for Felix to assume Jamie had fallen back to sleep, but when he glanced away from his hand stroking Jamie's skin, he found Jamie watching him intently.

Jamie reached out to touch Felix's belly, and his thumb caught on the flakes of dried come still clinging to Felix's skin from earlier. "How can you look so serious and so filthy at the same time?" Jamie slid his hand lower, drawing invisible patterns across the taut skin of Felix's hip and thigh. "Tell me what's going on in that head of yours."

Felix's breath hitched as Jamie's fingers skirted around his cock before sliding back up to settle on his hip. Nothing would be happening down there yet, but the proximity of Jamie's hand sent a shiver through him regardless. He raised his eyebrows, and Jamie smiled back.

"Couldn't resist when you're lying there all naked and on display." Jamie pushed up to match Felix's position, propping himself up with his elbow. "What are you going to do now about Weston?"

The question caught Felix by surprise, although he should probably have expected it after yesterday. He sighed and collapsed onto his back, looking up at the ceiling. "Nothing. I'm done with all that."

"Really?"

The scepticism in Jamie's voice didn't bother Felix half as much as it would have done a few days ago. Nick and Adam had been right, he'd held on to his anger and frustration for far too long, and it hadn't done him any favours. But he hadn't actually accepted it until that moment.

"Yeah." He turned his head to find Jamie frowning at him. "Karl Weston *is* a shady motherfucker. I've not changed my mind about that. And even if he never laid a hand on Jason, I do think he was in some way responsible for what happened to him."

"So why—"

"Because nothing I do will bring Jason back. Weston is never going to be connected to his death, and clinging to the hate and the anger is taking over my life and helping no one, least of all Jason." It hurt to talk about this, but Felix had never stopped to admit any of it before. "I tried to help him, so many fucking times, but he refused to listen and made some spectacularly bad decisions. I want to remember him how he was before all that shit, and I can't do that if I'm constantly focusing on his death."

Felix closed his eyes and covered his face with his hands. He felt lighter than he had in months. Saying it out loud for someone else to witness gave it more credence, and for once it felt like more than empty words.

Jamie had yet to say anything, and Felix had the sinking feeling that his decision wasn't what Jamie wanted to hear. He couldn't blame him. Until now, they'd been united in their grief and anger, both wanting answers. Finding someone who understood had been a relief for Felix, and he was certain Jamie felt the same. But if Felix let go of all that....

He rolled onto his side again, and had all his suspicions confirmed when he saw the expression on Jamie's face. Instead of the sleepy content from before, he looked as though he'd just had the rug pulled out from under him. "Hey." Cupping Jamie's cheek before he could move away, Felix leaned in and kissed him.

Jamie kissed Felix back readily enough, but it had an air of desperation and finality about it that made Felix want to wrap his arms around him and keep him there. Sure enough, as soon as Felix drew back, Jamie shuffled away from him and sat up.

Facing the wall, he clutched the quilt around his waist, self-conscious in a way he hadn't been before. "I think I should go."

"Wait, why?" Felix grabbed hold of Jamie's wrist to stop him from getting out of bed. "Because of what I just said?" He scrambled up, refusing to let go until he got close enough to wrap his arms around Jamie's shoulders and pull him back against his chest.

Jamie tensed, but after a couple of seconds, he relaxed into Felix and let his head fall back onto Felix's shoulder. "It's just…."

"Just what?" Felix had a good idea what the problem was, but he wanted Jamie to say it.

"I don't know." He reached up to hold onto Felix's arms. "I know it's stupid, but I feel like—" Jamie blew out a harsh breath, his body tense again. "Never mind. Like I said, I'm being ridiculous."

"You feel left behind?" Felix offered.

"Sort of." He was obviously struggling to find the right words, so Felix gave him an encouraging kiss on the side of his neck. Jamie finally said, "You've decided to move on—which is great, don't get me wrong—and I feel like I should do the same, but I can't and I—"

"For fuck's sake, Jamie." Felix squeezed him tight to get his full attention. "Jason died eleven months ago. It still hurts, it always will, but I can deal with it better now. You've only just lost Michael." He waited for Jamie to protest Michael's death as he always did, but Jamie said nothing. "It's going to feel shit for a long time."

Jamie shuddered in his arms and Felix gently shifted position, pulling Jamie back down onto the bed to lie half on Felix's chest. "I don't want you to go. Okay?"

Tugging the quilt up over them, Felix began to stroke up and down Jamie's back as he'd done before. Slowly the tension seeped out of Jamie's body; each sweep of Felix's fingers relaxed him further until Jamie felt like a dead weight.

"Okay."

Felix smiled to himself, kissed the top of Jamie's head, and closed his eyes.

The next time Felix woke, two things became apparent very quickly. He was absolutely starving and dying for a piss. Jamie had his arm slung across Felix's belly, pressing on his bladder and making matters ten times worse. Felix's stomach made a noise loud enough to wake the dead, and he wasn't at all surprised when Jamie stirred.

"Shift over, I need to get up." He shoved at Jamie's arm, hopping out of bed as soon as Jamie rolled onto his back. The sun shone brightly outside, but this bedroom didn't catch it in the afternoon and the air was cool after lying tucked up in bed with Jamie. Felix hurried to the bathroom, rubbing his hands up and down his arms to fend off the chill. Once he'd been to the loo, he washed his hands, gave his teeth a quick brush, and climbed back into bed. Then he put his feet on Jamie's legs to warm them up.

"Jesus, your feet are freezing!"

Jamie tried to move his legs away, but Felix rolled on top of him and pinned him in place face down on the mattress. "I know, but you're all warm." He wiggled closer and nuzzled at the back of Jamie's neck. The new position had the added bonus of bringing Felix's cock into close proximity to Jamie's arse. He couldn't resist flexing his hips, rubbing his rapidly hardening length between Jamie's cheeks. The loud rumble of Felix's stomach made him freeze midthrust, and he felt the vibrations of Jamie laughing underneath him.

"Hungry?" Jamie asked between chuckles.

"Bloody starving." Felix nipped the top of Jamie's shoulder and smiled against his warm skin. "It's all this exercise."

Jamie tried to push himself up, but Felix was way too heavy for him to move. All he succeeded in doing was pressing his arse more firmly against Felix's groin. "Shall we go downstairs and make something?"

Jamie's voice was breathy and ragged, and Felix's wasn't much better when he replied. "If you want."

He rolled his hips as Jamie pushed up, and neither spoke for the next few seconds. Food no longer seemed a priority and Felix easily ignored his empty belly, too focused on the slide of his cock along Jamie's crease. *It would be so easy to spread Jamie's thighs wide and fuck him.* As soon as the thought entered his head, it was all Felix could concentrate on. He slipped his hands under Jamie's shoulders, the tight grip eliciting a low moan.

Felix leaned in, his lips brushing the shell of Jamie's ear. "Are you sore?" He trailed soft kisses on the smooth skin down his neck. Jamie shivered. "I really want to fuck you again."

The answer to that was another soft moan, but Felix needed him to say the words. "Jamie?"

Jamie turned his head to the side so his mouth wasn't squashed into the pillows. "A little sore, but it's fine."

Fine? Felix stilled above him. No way was he going to hurt Jamie just to get off. "How about I blow you instead?" He pushed up on his hands, ready to roll off to the side, but Jamie's hand shot back and clamped onto Felix's thigh, hard.

Glaring as best he could from his position on the bed, Jamie narrowed his eyes and squeezed his hand to keep Felix from moving. "I might not be as tough as you, soldier boy, but I'm not going to break. Obviously when I said fine, I meant horny as fuck, so get yourself ready and put your cock in me. *Please.*"

The *please* had Felix grinning against Jamie's shoulder, but the rest of the sentence had him hard and aching. This bossy version of Jamie took him by surprise and was hot as hell. "Okay," he whispered, pushing himself up again, and this time Jamie let him go.

Felix had the condom on in record time—for once it hadn't taken him an age to find them in his drawer. Jamie snagged a pillow and thrust it under his hips, spreading his legs wide for Felix to get between them.

But Felix lay down next to him at first, draping one leg over Jamie's and shuffling in close. He had one hand clasped in Jamie's alongside his head, while sliding the slick fingers on the other back and forth over his hole.

Pressing down hard enough for the tip of his finger to slide inside, Felix leaned in until his mouth was next to Jamie's ear again. "It's *ex*-soldier boy." He slid his finger in farther and withdrew it slowly, only to push two back in its place, moving them steadily in and out until he had Jamie writhing and cursing into the pillow. "And I think you're plenty tough enough."

Jamie's huff of laughter cut off abruptly as Felix removed his hand, climbed between Jamie's spread legs and thrust into him with one sure stroke.

"Fuck!" Jamie yelled it into the pillow, and for one split second Felix faltered, wondering if he'd hurt him after all. But then Jamie fisted the sheets, fingers curling in tight. "Come on, fuck me."

All the uncertainty fell away with Jamie's gruff commands, and Felix grinned, drew his hips back, and gave Jamie what he wanted. Soft grunts and muttered pleas spurred him on. He wanted to see himself fucking into Jamie, wanted to watch his cock slide inside him again and again, so he kneeled up, taking Jamie with him until he was on all fours.

Felix slid his hands from Jamie's hips, guided them down over his sweat-slicked arse, and thumbed Jamie's rim as he slowed his thrusts. Without much thought about what he was doing, Felix rubbed the pad of one thumb up and down in time with each stroke, pressing harder each time.

"Do it," Jamie gritted out, pushing back against him.

Felix eased his thumb in alongside his dick and Jamie swore, letting his head drop down between his shoulders. Felix couldn't tear his gaze away, but the sight of his thumb and his cock stretching Jamie like that had his balls drawing tight with the urge to fuck him hard and fast.

He pulled his thumb out and grabbed Jamie's hips, his rhythm all shot to shit as he slammed into him over and over. "Fuck, I'm gonna come." Felix was too far gone to stop it, but Jamie must have heard the desperation in his voice and he fell forward onto one elbow, shoving his other arm underneath to jerk himself off.

Jamie came first, and the sudden tightness around Felix pulled him over almost straight after. He leaned heavily onto Jamie's back, forcing him to collapse down to the bed with a grunt and a short bubble of laughter.

"I take it back," Jamie mumbled into Felix's pillow. "I'm not tough, and you're crushing me." He reached back and slapped half-heartedly at Felix's thigh. "Off."

With great effort, Felix pulled out, rolled onto his back, and disposed of the condom in the bin next to the bed. His legs ached, his arms ached, and his stomach felt like it was about to eat itself. He smiled to himself, happier than he remembered being in months. When was the last time he'd been this exhausted from sex, or this comfortable with the person he'd had it with? The fact that he had no idea said it all.

Jamie stirred beside him. Felix glanced over to see him lying there with his eyes closed and a contented smile. For the first time since Felix had met him, there was no lingering sadness there, none of the haunting sense of loss that Jamie usually carried with him. Felix didn't think for one second it had gone; it was just a short reprieve from the horrors of the past couple of weeks. Jamie looked younger without all the worry, and Felix wanted to curl around him and enjoy him while he could.

This sense of contentment wouldn't last, Felix knew that well, and with a sharp jolt, he realised the rest of it wouldn't either. Jamie would be gone in a few days, and would take all of this with him. Felix wasn't sure when he'd got used to having Jamie around, but he was going to miss him when he left.

"What's wrong?" Jamie's voice snapped him out of his introspection.

Felix shook his head, forcing the dark thoughts away, and plastered a smile on his face. Since when did he wear his emotions so openly? "Nothing. I think my stomach is about to revolt at the lack of food. Let's go and shower, and then I'll make us lunch. Yeah?"

Jamie eyed him curiously for a moment, as though not totally buying Felix's answer, but he let it go and followed Felix to the bathroom.

They ate a late lunch of loaded sandwiches with huge mugs of tea, then spent the rest of the afternoon cuddled on the settee watching rubbish on the telly.

Felix insisted on getting some fresh air after a couple of hours. The niggling worry from earlier had got under his skin and made him restless.

Usually he was upfront about sex, both parties knowing what to expect. But he and Jamie had just happened. Despite only knowing him for a short while, Felix liked him, and under different circumstances, he'd like to have seen where this could go. But logically he knew this was only a holiday fling; they were both leaving soon, so what else could it be?

He'd had this conversation with Nick and Adam before they left. They'd liked Jamie too and said he was good for Felix, and had heavily hinted that he should keep seeing him after Jamie went back to Nottingham. At Felix's protests, Nick pointed out how often he'd been away from his wife in the years they'd been together.

Whatever. Felix wasn't Nick, and who knew what Jamie's thoughts were on the whole thing. Determined to enjoy the rest of the weekend and ignore everything else until he had to deal with it, Felix made Jamie put his jacket on and dragged him up the hill past his aunt and uncle's house.

"Is all this land theirs?" Jamie held his arms out wide and pointed at the fields surrounding them on three sides. The wind had picked up, and it kept blowing his hair into his eyes. He shoved it out of the way with a frustrated huff, making Felix smile.

"No, not all of it." Felix pointed out which fields belonged to their neighbours and what they grew in them, and Jamie nodded along, taking it all in.

The walk was all uphill, and twenty minutes in, Jamie stopped and put his hands on his thighs, breathing heavily. "Christ. Either I'm out of shape or you sapped all my energy." He glanced up at Felix. "How much farther?"

Felix slapped him on the back, catching his arm when he stumbled. "Such a lightweight. It's not like you had to do any of the work earlier, you just lie there and—"

"Fuck off!" Jamie tried to swat Felix's arse but Felix easily avoided him, laughing.

"Come on, it's only a bit farther, I promise."

Felix pulled Jamie close as he stood straight, and kissed him until Jamie was breathless again.

"That's not exactly helping, you know." Jamie looped his arms around Felix's neck and rested his head on his shoulder.

They stayed like that until Jamie sighed and stepped back. "Lead the way, then."

Chapter Thirteen

Soon the green fields gave way to rocky ground with heather and gorse dotted here and there. The roar of the sea was audible now, and the salty air filled Jamie's lungs as they walked.

Felix grabbed Jamie's hand and tugged him close. "Watch your step."

Before Jamie could ask why, they crested the hill and—"Oh." He immediately took a step back from what looked like a sheer drop down to the sea, but Felix stopped him going any farther.

"It's safe. This bit drops away steeply, but it flattens out about ten foot below. Look." He led Jamie along a path to the left where the land curved, giving them a better vantage point. Sure enough, from this angle he could see where it sloped down to a small rocky plateau and then dropped again down to the sea. Felix sat on the rough grass and tugged Jamie down with him.

The view was breathtaking. The low-hanging sun had turned orange in the evening sky; its warm glow bathed the blue-grey of the Atlantic below. Everything felt fresh and alive up there; no wonder Felix liked it so much. This past week had seemed more like a month. Jamie had got used to the sea air and being outdoors all the time, and he was going to miss it. They sat in companionable silence, watching the waves roll in and crash onto the rocks below, and Jamie's thoughts inevitably turned to Michael. Was he out there somewhere, his body lost forever?

As much as he hated to admit it, Jamie knew deep down they might never know for sure what had happened to him. At this point they couldn't mourn properly either. Without proof Michael was dead, Jamie knew he'd always hold out a sliver of hope his brother would somehow turn up one day.

Jamie's eyes prickled with unshed tears and he blinked them away rapidly.

"You okay?" Felix shuffled closer and wrapped an arm around Jamie's shoulders.

"Yeah." Jamie swallowed back the flood of emotion threatening to overwhelm him, but his voice still came out low and rough. "Just thinking."

"About Michael?"

Jamie glanced up quickly, surprised at Felix's insight. He nodded.

"Don't look so shocked. It doesn't take a genius to figure out why you suddenly look so sad."

"I really fucking miss him."

Felix held him tighter. "I know." He didn't say anything else, just held Jamie close as they sat there watching the sea roll in and the sun set in the distance.

The last rays disappeared, leaving a chill in the air, and Jamie shivered.

It felt like an ending.

Sunday morning arrived far too soon. Jamie lay on his back, staring up at the white ceiling of Felix's bedroom. He'd planned on going home tomorrow and had already told his parents he'd be round for tea. The cottage was paid for until a week on

Wednesday, so in theory he had over another week if he wanted, but he needed to get back to work.

Felix stirred in his sleep next to him, rolling over and sliding an arm over Jamie's waist. The warmth from his naked body made Jamie sigh softly. He could so easily get used to this… and wasn't that bloody typical?

The last few years he'd been so focused on work—going self-employed had been a risk—that a relationship was out of the question. He hadn't had the time to spare for relationships, and figured he had years ahead of him for that sort of stuff.

Michael's disappearance—*death,* his mind corrected—put things in perspective. No one knew for certain how long they had. If Jamie continued to put off getting involved with someone, he might never get the chance.

And then there was Felix. Someone whom he wanted to let in, to spend time with and see how things panned out. But Jamie lived in Nottingham, and Felix was moving to Reading. They'd known each other a week. That was hardly a strong foundation for a long-distance relationship.

Fuck it all.

He put a hand over Felix's and twined their fingers together. All this might be wishful thinking on Jamie's part. They hadn't talked about this. It might be just sex for Felix, a holiday fling; probably was, in all likelihood. Just because Jamie had got attached so quickly didn't mean Felix had. Leaving without at least discussing it wasn't something Jamie was prepared to do, though. Maybe a few months ago or even a few *weeks* ago, he would have, but not now. As soon as Felix woke up, they were going to talk.

Jamie was in no hurry for that to happen, so he closed his eyes and dozed with Felix wrapped around him.

When Jamie woke again, he opened his eyes to find Felix sat up next to him with a book in his lap.

Felix glanced over as Jamie turned on his side. "Morning."

"Morning." Jamie's voice was rough, while Felix sounded like he'd been awake for hours. "What time is it?"

Felix checked his watch. "Ten thirty-seven."

"Shit, didn't realise it was that late." Since Michael went missing, Jamie had had trouble sleeping past six or seven. He yawned, making his jaw click. Apparently he was still tired.

Putting his book aside, Felix slid down the bed until he was level with Jamie. "We did have a late night, remember." His gaze dropped to Jamie's bare chest and then lower to where he'd pushed the quilt down around his hips. "I'm not surprised we slept late."

Jamie reached under the covers and palmed his morning wood. It wouldn't take much to get him fully hard, and thinking about Felix blowing him last night would easily do the trick, but there was a conversation they needed to have. Lying face-to-face in Felix's bed seemed more conducive to honesty and openness than anywhere else Jamie could think of.

With a sigh, he let go of his cock and took hold of Felix's hand. He watched Felix's expression change as he realised Jamie had something serious to say.

"What?"

Jamie had started this conversation so many ways in his head, but none of them felt right. He went with bluntness. "I'm going back up to Nottingham tomorrow."

Felix stilled, his fingers tightening around Jamie's. When he spoke, his voice was soft and steady, almost matter-of-fact. "The cottage is paid up until the thirtieth."

Jamie couldn't tell if Felix was upset, relieved, or not bothered. "I know, but I've already stayed longer than I planned. My parents are expecting me home tomorrow."

"Oh." Felix looked down at their joined hands, then shifted onto his back with a heavy sigh. He kept hold of Jamie's fingers, though, bringing their hands onto his chest.

Jamie bit his lip. *Now or never*. "I don't want this to end. I know it won't be easy, but I don't want to leave here and never see you again."

Felix turned his head to face him, and Jamie's stomach dropped at the pained look in his eyes. "Jamie… *shit*."

Ah, here it comes. Jamie braced himself for the "it was fun, but that's all it was" speech.

It must have shown on his face because Felix shifted onto his side again. "Don't look at me like that."

Jamie scoffed. "How should I look? You're about to tell me 'thanks, but no thanks,' so I think I'm allowed to be a bit pissed off."

"I haven't even said anything yet!"

"Okay. Tell me I'm wrong, then." Jamie snatched his hand out of Felix's grasp when he didn't reply. "Tell me you want to keep seeing me when we both leave here, and find out where this" — he gestured between the two of them — "could lead."

Felix scrubbed a hand over his eyes. "You have your life back up north, and I'm still sorting myself out. I don't know yet if I'll stay in Reading or even if this new job will work out. It's not as simple as you're making out."

"It's exactly that simple. You're the one who's making it difficult." Suddenly Jamie wanted to be anywhere other than in the same bed with him. "You know as well as I do that life is too short not to take chances. I like you, Felix. These past few days have been some of the best I can remember having, and not because of all the sex. I have no idea if we'd be good together long-term. I agree the circumstances are shitty, but I also know I'll regret it if I walk away without at least trying, and I don't want any more regrets if I can help it."

Felix continued to stare at him, not saying anything, and the fight simply drained out of him. He'd said his piece, laid his cards on the table. Now it was up to Felix.

Jamie sat up and pulled the quilt over his lap. "So." He waited until Felix was looking at him before continuing. "Do you want to see me again or not?"

"Jamie. I—" Felix started to reach for him, then obviously thought better of it. "—I can't. I'm sorry." He looked torn, as if the words weren't what he wanted to say at all, and Jamie willed him to take them back and change his mind, but he didn't say anything else.

Jamie felt the silence like a chill in the air, and a coldness settled inside him. He needed to get out of there. "Okay, then."

Not caring that he was naked, Jamie pushed the covers off, got out of bed, and started to look for his clothes. He wanted to get dressed and go now.

"Jamie, wait. Let me explain."

Felix made a grab for him, but Jamie ducked out of his reach. "Look." Jamie tried for calm and controlled, only 50 percent convinced he pulled it off. "I wanted to see you again, which is why I asked the question. You obviously don't feel the same, and that's fine. We didn't make any promises when we started this. You don't need to justify your answer. I'm disappointed, but I'll get over it." He pulled on his jeans and then his T-shirt, hoping Felix would leave it at that. He had no desire to listen to all the reasons Felix didn't want him.

"But I—"

Jamie spun around to face him. "Please stop." He spotted his socks under the corner of the bed and bent down to pick them up. "Don't make this any harder for me. You've already shot me down." He tried for a smile but was pretty sure he failed miserably. "I just want to leave with some dignity intact."

Felix watched him struggle to put his socks on while standing, and eventually nodded. "I'm sorry."

"I know." Jamie walked over to the bed and sat down, not wanting to leave it like this. They'd shared a lot in such a short time, and if it had to end, he'd rather it wasn't on a sour note. Felix had been there for him when he needed someone. "Thanks for the last few days. I'm glad I met you."

"Me too." Felix reached for Jamie's hand, and Jamie let him take it this time. "Goodbye, Jamie."

"Bye." Jamie leaned in and kissed him quickly before getting up and walking out of the bedroom.

A lead weight settled in his stomach as he descended the stairs. Part of him had been convinced Felix would say yes. The last couple of days had been so easy, Jamie felt sure it wasn't one-sided. Either he'd misread Felix's actions or—*for fuck's sake!* He was overthinking things again. None of that mattered in the end. Felix didn't want to stay in touch, and that was that.

Jamie slipped on his shoes in the hallway, grabbed his jacket and keys, and pulled the front door shut behind him. It closed with a loud *click* that sounded so final, Jamie's chest constricted. He shouldn't be this upset about someone he hardly knew; it was stupid.

But he was.

The feeling that something good had slipped through his fingers plagued him all the way back to the cottage. By the time he pulled up in front of it, Jamie was almost convinced Felix was full of shit and his reasons for not at least trying to have a relationship were ridiculous. The hurt coursing through Jamie slowly turned to anger, and he was half tempted to turn around, go back, and convince Felix to give it a go. If it didn't work out, then fine. What would it hurt to try?

He slammed his hands against the steering wheel and growled in frustration. Why did everything have to be such a fucking struggle? Jamie yanked the keys out of the ignition and got out before he changed his mind. No way did he want to beg Felix, and that would probably happen if he went back.

Slamming the car door made him feel slightly better, and he stalked across the drive to the front door, attempting to breathe deeply in and out, and let some of his frustration drain away. If Felix didn't want to take a chance on him, then fuck him.

Most of Michael's things were already packed. Jamie zipped up the bags and carried them downstairs, leaving the sketchpad out. After checking the bedroom, bathroom, and the downstairs to make sure he'd got everything, Jamie grabbed Michael's sketchbook and took it outside.

Sitting in the shade, he flipped open the book and began to look through his brother's drawings. Carefully, so as not to damage any of the pages, he worked his way through some of the older drawings. The feelings they evoked were bittersweet, and he smiled with tears in his eyes remembering Michael describing them in animated detail.

When he reached the newer drawings, Jamie's breath caught. There were ones of the cottage — half-finished but still beautiful. On the following pages, he'd drawn smaller pictures of the rocks and water, the same view Jamie would see if he walked out past the end of the garden.

The next page held the first drawing of the beach where he'd disappeared. Jamie ran his hand along the edges. Even on paper, the sea looked rough and dangerous. Michael had drawn the waves crashing onto the beach, colliding with the rocks and sending spray high into the air. The next page held something similar. The last thing the water looked was inviting.

Jesus, Michael. Why did you go into that fucking sea?

It still didn't make sense. *Will it ever?*

Wiping away the tears that spilled over, he then turned the page, expecting more of the same but—

"Oh my God!"

Jamie sat bolt upright, nearly dropping the pad onto the ground in his haste. This time, instead of the sea, Michael had drawn the hill and the path leading up to the house, with only the top of the house visible. That was the view from the sand.

The next page had a better view of the house. Michael must have walked up the path to get that. Something caught Jamie's eye, and he leaned in closer. Michael had drawn a lone figure standing on the wrap-around balcony. The face wasn't recognisable, but that had to be Karl Weston, right?

Jamie's heart rate picked up, his hands shaking slightly as he turned the next page.

Jesus Christ.

Staring back at him was a close-up drawing of the man leaning on the balcony. He grabbed his phone, fumbling as his shaking intensified. He already knew it, but one Google search later and his mouth went dry.

The man in the drawing was unmistakably Karl Weston. How had the police missed that?

A jumble of emotions rushed through him, but only one thing stuck in his head: Michael must have met him. To get close enough for a drawing that detailed, Michael had to have sat on that balcony with him. According to the police, Weston said he'd never met Michael.

That lying bastard.

He said he'd never even seen him on the beach. Weston might have an alibi for the day Michael disappeared, but Jamie held the proof that the rest of his story was utter fucking rubbish. Maybe the alibi was too. Jamie didn't know details of Weston's whereabouts that weekend; maybe he'd got people to lie for him.

What the fuck did he do now? His first thought was to call Felix, and he got as far as scrolling through his contacts to his name before stopping. Felix was done with Weston — and Jamie too now. He didn't need dragging back into this. Besides, this wasn't something anyone but the police should be involved with.

The officers in charge of his brother's case had given him a card, and Jamie pulled out his wallet, hoping he hadn't tossed it out. Finding it lodged behind his bank card, he quickly dialled the number with unsteady fingers and waited for it to connect.

It rang and rang... Jamie was two seconds away from hanging up when someone answered.

"Bodmin Police Station, how can I help you?"

"Hi. I'm trying to get through to Detective Brierley. I have some information on my missing brother."

The officer on the other end took Jamie's details, obviously recognising his name, and he apologised, saying that Detective Brierley was in court for the day. Jamie silently cursed. His gaze drifted back to the drawing on the table next to him.

"I can take a message and pass it on, or you can come into the station tomorrow morning and see him in person?"

"Can I do both?" Jamie asked, desperate to tell someone what he'd found. To him it felt like a huge breakthrough in his brother's case, but the guy he was speaking to wasn't as interested as Jamie thought he should be. To say it was frustrating was an understatement.

"Certainly, sir."

So Jamie described the drawing he'd found and explained his theories about Michael having met Weston. The officer assured him he would pass on the information as soon as the detective was available, and that Brierley would definitely be in touch later.

After thanking him and hanging up, Jamie sat back in his seat; his leg bounced with nervous energy. He'd done all he could, and it was up to the police now. Far too restless to sit still any longer, he stood and walked down to the end of the garden and out through the gate.

The view took him by surprise every time he saw it, but today the calmness of the sea only served to make him more agitated. Jamie wanted to see the waves crashing into the shoreline, because that was how he felt inside.

After he'd finally accepted that his brother had met with a tragic accident and no foul play was involved, that picture had surfaced and brought with it a whole slew of doubts. If Weston had lied about knowing Michael, what else had he lied about? Of course it might have nothing whatsoever to do with the case... Weston could have lied to avoid being questioned further by police, and be totally innocent. There was nothing in that photo to suggest Michael hadn't accidentally drowned, but... Weston had lied.

That was the part that had Jamie's instincts screaming at him. Karl Weston knew something about his brother's disappearance; he could feel it in his bones. Christ, he hoped court finished early today.

Four hours later, Jamie had packed up his things, leaving only the essentials out for that night and the following morning, and stacked them in the middle of the lounge with Michael's. But still no call from the police. It looked like it would be morning now before he spoke to anyone. Maybe he should stay a day longer?

He fiddled with his phone, turning it over in his hands and willing it to ring.

Could he go back home now that he'd found that drawing? His curiosity said no, but realistically there was nothing to keep him here. The police would inform his parents if they had any new information about Michael's disappearance. Jamie had no reason to stay.

Michael was gone, and Jamie needed to accept that—he *had* accepted that, he just hated leaving things unfinished.

The sketchpad sat open on the coffee table. Jamie had been looking at it on and off all afternoon. Weston had a small smile on his face as he looked out to sea. If he'd let Michael draw him like that, then did it mean they'd been friends? Jamie would give anything to know about his brother's last few days. That drawing was dated September 3, the Thursday before he disappeared. Why had Michael never mentioned Weston in his calls or texts?

Christ, the not knowing was driving him crazy. He just wanted the truth. Was that so much to ask?

Jamie had his keys in his hand before the idea had fully formed in his mind. What could Weston do to him in broad daylight? This was Cornwall, for God's sake, not some dodgy area of London. Jamie had been a reporter; he knew how to ask questions. Weston might not answer them, but Jamie was sick and tired of sitting on his arse doing nothing. He would go, ask about the picture, probably get the door slammed in his face and be threatened with solicitors, and then leave.

Grabbing his jacket, Jamie locked up the cottage and got in his car. He wasn't entirely reckless, though. Felix might be the last person he wanted to contact, but he was the only option.

Jamie quickly typed out a text.

Found a drawing that Michael did of Weston. On my way to the house to ask Weston about it.

He pressed Send, then turned it off. Undoubtedly, Felix would have something to say about that, but Jamie was in no mood to listen to it. With any luck he'd be there and back before Felix even read the text.

Chapter Fourteen

Felix flinched as the front door slammed shut. He lay on his back with his eyes closed, listening to the sounds of Jamie getting into his car and driving away. "Fuck!"

His voice was too loud in the near silence of his bedroom, and Jamie's sudden absence was like a physical ache. He pulled the quilt up over his head to block it all out, but the bed smelled like sex and Felix quickly shoved the cover off him again, hitting the mattress in frustration.

It had been the right decision. Felix's last proper relationship was a long while ago, but he remembered how it had fizzled away to nothing with all the time he spent away from home. He and Jamie had known each other for about a week; how could they try for a long-distance relationship after such a short time together? Felix liked Jamie, he liked him a lot, but that didn't mean they'd be good together in the long run. Felix had a new life to start, and that was going to be hard enough after so many years in the Army; the added complication of a new relationship would be asking for trouble.

Besides, Jamie had dealt with enough heartbreak these last few weeks. Why add to it by starting something that was destined to fail and hurt them both? Felix didn't want to be another person who caused him pain.

He rubbed at the stubble on his jaw, which was itchy after not shaving for a few days, and finally acknowledged the niggling voice at the back of his mind.

If it was the right decision, why doesn't it feel like it?

Felix spent the rest of the morning going through what he needed to do when he started his new job in October. As a self-employed contractor, he already had an accountant and his company set up. He had his company bank account and credit card, which always made him shake his head. He was both the director and the sole employee; it was weird. But it was what the taxman wanted, so that was what he'd done.

He started to read up on the company he would be working for and what the job might entail. Project management was pretty standard in any company, but Felix would be glad when he had the first contract under his belt. Civvy Street was going to be an adjustment, no matter how much prep he did.

Struggling to concentrate on the words in front of him, his mind kept wandering back to Jamie and what he'd said before he left.

Life is too short not to take chances....

Felix thought about the friends he'd lost in combat, and *Jason*. Life *was* too fucking short, and Felix should know that better than most. *Bollocks.* He'd behaved like a right arsehole. Jamie was the best thing to happen to him in a long while, and he'd let him walk out the door without so much as a word of protest. All because the alternative would mean hard work, compromise, and the risk of failure. None of which Felix was a stranger to, for God's sake.

It might suck at times being so many miles apart, but Felix had given up without even trying, and that was so unlike him he felt appalled at himself. Two months out of the Army and he was already a quitter. Jesus, he needed a slap.

His phone lay on the bedside table and he snatched it up. Shit, what if Jamie had left already? He'd said he wasn't leaving until tomorrow, but what if Felix had made him want to go sooner?

The screen was black and it stayed that way when he pressed the power button. "Oh for fuck's sake!" Of all the times to have run out of charge.

He shot out of bed, shrugging into yesterday's jeans and T-shirt, not caring whether they were clean or not. Now he'd made his mind up to go after Jamie, he couldn't get there soon enough. He'd charge his phone on the way.

Thank God the roads were empty because Felix wasn't paying all that much attention to driving, too busy thinking of what he'd say to Jamie when he got to the cottage. The journey went way too quickly; nothing convincing had sprung to mind by the time he took the turning onto the driveway.

His train of thought stopped abruptly when he pulled up in front and saw a police car parked outside instead of Jamie's Honda. Sweat ran down the back of Felix's neck as the late-afternoon sun shone brightly through the car windows. A chill swept through him and dread filled him up from the inside. As if moving in slow motion, Felix got out and walked over to the police car, stopping in his tracks as the car door swung open.

"Hey, Felix. I've been trying to call you." Detective Mark Brierley frowned as he stood and leaned against the door frame. Felix had gone to secondary school with him, though Mark looked a far cry from the gangly teen he used to be.

Felix gestured vaguely over at his car. "My phone was out of charge." Just to prove him wrong, he heard the telltale beep of a text message. "Obviously not anymore." Glancing at the cottage, then back at Brierley, he said, "What are you doing here?"

"Mr. Matthews called the station this morning. Said he had some new information regarding his brother's case."

"Oh?" Felix felt a stab of irritation at being left out of the loop. Jamie was pissed off with him, and obviously with good reason, but surely he would have shared something to do with his brother's disappearance. That he hadn't hurt more than Felix wanted to let on. He shoved his hands in his pockets, trying for nonchalance. "Why were you calling me, then?"

"To see if you knew where he was." Brierley shut his car door and locked it. He fixed Felix with a knowing look. "Rumour has it you and Mr. Matthews are quite friendly."

"Is that so?" How the hell had anyone seen them together? Felix had always hated the way everyone wanted to know your business. "Well, sorry, but I have no idea where he is." His phone beeped again with the unread text and Felix pointed over his shoulder. "Want me to call him?"

"I've already tried twice and it went to voicemail, but be my guest." Brierley shrugged, a small smile creeping over his face. "Maybe he'll answer if it's you."

Felix ignored him, turned, and walked over to where his driver's door stood open. His phone lay on the passenger seat, and he ducked inside to grab it, stopping half over the centre console when he saw he had a text from Jamie. "Shit."

He quickly thumbed opened the message as he shuffled back out of the car and straightened up.

"What's wrong?" Brierley came over to stand in front of him. "You look like you've seen a ghost."

Felix barely heard him through the rush of *no-no-no-no-no* running through his head. How could Jamie be so fucking stupid? After all he'd heard about Karl Weston this weekend. Not all of it was Felix's paranoia. Adam and Nick had both told Jamie that Weston was bad news. What the hell was he thinking going over there alone? Suddenly he felt sick and put a hand on the roof of his car.

"Felix?" All the gentle teasing had disappeared from Brierley's voice, replaced by the no-nonsense tone Felix associated with policemen.

Wordlessly, Felix turned the phone, showing him Jamie's message. He waited while Brierley read it, tapping his fingers on the car.

"Christ," Brierley exclaimed. "I guess that was what he wanted to show me. How the hell did we miss that? Doesn't Matthews realise he's interfering with our investigation by going over there?"

Felix wasn't sure if he expected an answer or not, but he was going to get one. Dialling Jamie's number with one hand, he glanced up at Mark. "Sod your investigation. Karl Weston is dangerous. Jamie might be in serious trouble if he's back at the house."

The call went straight to voicemail. "For God's sake, Jamie."

"Look, Felix. I know how you feel about Weston. Hell, the whole station does after we interviewed you about Michael Matthews's disappearance. But he's never done anything to warrant our attention out here. Not so much as a speeding ticket. And unfortunately, there's no law against being an arrogant so-and-so. Jamie shouldn't have gone over there, but I doubt he's in any danger. Weston will probably just tell him to get lost."

Felix pocketed his phone and moved to climb in his car, but Mark's hand on his shoulder stopped him.

"Where do you think you're going?"

Felix glared at him incredulously. "To Weston's house."

Brierley rolled his eyes. "But I just told you—"

"Did you read Jamie's text?"

"Yes, but—"

"Jamie told me Weston said he'd never met Michael. But if Michael drew a fucking picture of him, then he must have."

"We already questioned him about Michael Matthews. Mr. Weston has witnesses that put him in London all day Saturday. And we searched his house. There was nothing there. I really need to see that drawing before we go making accusations."

Felix scrubbed a hand over his short hair, wishing he had something to grab hold of. "Look, we're wasting time. Jamie could be over there right now. I appreciate you're in a difficult position, but I'm not. And I'm going over there."

"Fuck." Brierley looked torn. "If I get into trouble over this, I'm having you arrested."

Felix managed a grim smile. "Deal." He went to climb in his car, but Brierley stopped him again. "What now?"

Brierley waved his keys in Felix's face. "We'll take mine, make it an official enquiry."

Felix nodded and followed him to his car. When we get there" — he glanced over at Felix as he pulled on his seat belt — "you need to stay in the car. Understood?"

Not likely. "Of course."

Brierley shook his head as he reversed. "At least stay put until I talk to whoever's there." Felix grunted. Brierley cursed under his breath but didn't comment further.

They pulled away from the cottage in a spray of gravel and sped down the driveway towards the main road. At least Brierley wasn't hanging around and was taking Felix's concerns seriously. Felix sent Jamie a text telling him they were on their way — in the vain hope Jamie hadn't already got there — and he prayed his instincts were wrong this time.

Chapter Fifteen

Jamie missed the exit to Weston's house and had to turn around on a dirt track about two hundred metres past it. He slowed right down on the way back, not wanting to miss it a second time. Tapping his fingers on the steering wheel as he waited for a couple of cars to drive by so he could turn right, Jamie went over what he wanted to say. Assuming Weston was even there, of course.

According to Felix, Weston came and went unpredictably. Jamie couldn't decide whether he wanted him to be home or not. On the one hand, he desperately wanted to know what that drawing meant and how Weston was involved with Michael, but all Felix's warnings about him came rushing back as Jamie pulled onto the road that led to Weston's house.

He parked on the grass verge and sat there tapping his fingers on the steering wheel. Maybe he should wait and go see the police in the morning. But would they be interested? They'd already questioned Weston and the man had a solid alibi for when Michael disappeared.

He could ask his questions at the door, he didn't even have to set foot inside the house. Mind made up, he pulled out onto the road again. He needed to know the truth. Once a reporter….

A black X5 sat outside the house. Jamie parked alongside it, grabbed his phone, and got out.

Adrenaline coursed through him as he locked his car and walked up to the front door. The thought of finally getting some answers after so many sleepless nights wondering what had happened to Michael had his heart racing. He didn't expect to find out about the day Michael disappeared, but Weston must know something more than he'd told the police. Jamie hoped that by bringing up the drawing, Weston would admit to at least meeting Michael.

For a second Jamie wished he'd brought the drawing with him. With the evidence staring Weston in the face, he'd be hard put to deny it. But that drawing was all he had to show there was a connection between his brother and Karl Weston. It wasn't worth the risk of anything happening to it.

He slipped his phone into his jeans pocket as he approached the house, cursing as he remembered he'd turned the bloody thing off. What had he been thinking? Quickly fishing it out again and powering it back up, Jamie winced at the number of notifications that popped up. The last was a text from Felix, but before he had a chance to open it and read, the front door opened, startling him.

Karl Weston stepped out to meet him. "Can I help you?"

Jamie pocketed his phone again and straightened, meeting Weston's gaze with as much confidence as he could muster. "Yes, I think you can. My name's Jamie Matthews." If Weston recognised the name, he didn't react. "I wanted to talk to you about my brother, Michael."

Weston leaned casually against the door frame, blocking the entrance and definitely not about to invite Jamie inside. He shrugged. "Should that name mean something to me?"

Jamie clenched his fists at his sides. His phone buzzed, but he ignored it in favour of keeping eye contact with Weston. "Considering he was at your house a couple of days before he disappeared, I think so, yes."

A flicker of uncertainty flashed across Weston's face, replaced almost immediately with disinterest. Jamie's pulse quickened.

"I recognise the name, now I think about it. It was a tragic accident, and I'm sorry for your loss." Weston's voice suddenly developed a hard edge to it. "But like I told the police when they questioned me over a week ago, I never met your brother. You must be mistaken."

With a smile, Jamie took a step closer until they were within touching distance. Even though he'd been expecting it, hearing the lie come so easily set Jamie's teeth on edge. Anger welled up inside him, making him less cautious than he would have been otherwise. He shook his head. "You know; I don't think I am. You see, my brother was an artist. A bloody good one at that." He waited to see if Weston reacted to that bit of information, but either he didn't know Michael had drawn him or he had an impressive poker face. Considering everything Felix had said about him, Jamie was leaning towards the latter.

"And?"

"And he drew you." Excitement shot through him as Weston finally looked wrong-footed. He attempted to mask it quickly, but Jamie wanted to crow with victory because he'd seen it—Weston knew about the drawing.

"What makes you think that?" Weston stood up straight with his hands in his pockets.

Jamie couldn't help glancing down, hoping that was all he had in there. Not that he expected Weston to walk around his house with a gun or knife in his pocket, but with the amount of adrenaline pumping through Jamie's veins, his mind was working overtime. With an effort, he dragged his gaze back to Weston's and grinned. "Because I've seen it."

"That's impossible. I—" Weston clamped his mouth shut, immediately realising his error. He narrowed his eyes, and his expression turned cold and calculating. A shiver ran down Jamie's spine. "Why don't you come inside and we can discuss this somewhere more comfortable than on my doorstep?" He stepped back, making room for Jamie to go by him, and waited. Jamie hesitated. Weston raised his eyebrows, and Jamie had the feeling he was being mocked. "I thought you wanted some answers?"

Jamie nodded. "I do. But—"

"But what?" Weston put his arm out in a sweeping gesture. "You came to see me, and I'm inviting you inside my home, like any civilised person would do."

Fuck, Felix had made him paranoid. Jamie could easily imagine him shaking his head and telling Jamie he would be fucking crazy to go inside with Weston. The memory of Felix poked at the raw, tender place inside him, and Jamie shoved all thoughts of him aside for now. It was none of Felix's business anyway. "Lead the way."

Weston smiled at him. Jamie's reporter's instincts told him to tread carefully. Something about Weston's mannerisms pinged all his radars, and he glanced around warily as Weston stepped around him to close the front door. It slammed shut with a dull *thud* that sounded way too loud and menacing in the quiet of the hallway.

Jesus, he'd been out of the loop too long. Working at home all day had made him lose his sense of adventure. He never used to be this bad when he worked for the paper. *Get it together, Jamie.*

Weston led them through the large open-plan ground floor. The house seemed out of place with the old cottage-style buildings Jamie had seen along the coast, even more so when they went up the wooden staircase and saw the large picture windows of the living room. There the huge glass doors opened out onto a wrap-around balcony overlooking the sea. Jamie recognised it from Michael's drawing, and when Weston walked out and leaned against the railing—just as Michael had drawn him—Jamie knew it was a calculated move on his part.

Weston beckoned to him to come outside. "Don't you want to see the view?"

Jamie could see the view just fine from inside the living room, thank you very much. The balcony was only on the first floor, not all that high, but the glass barrier let him see exactly how far it was to the ground below. He didn't care if he was being paranoid now, Weston was ex-Army, and if he was anything like Felix, he could probably overpower Jamie quickly and easily. Going out onto that balcony would be a bad idea. "I can see it perfectly okay from here, thanks."

"Suit yourself." Weston shrugged as though he didn't give a shit either way, then turned his back to look out over the sea. The fitted T-shirt he wore clung to him like a second skin, accenting the muscles in his shoulders, his back, and the tops of his arms. Like Felix, Weston kept his hair short, but it didn't work for him in quite the same way. Or maybe Jamie was biased.

Weston glanced over at him, one hand tapping out a silent rhythm on the top of the rail. "Where's the drawing now?"

Jamie couldn't get a read on his mood, and he wondered if he should lie. His gut told him Weston would know, and what did he have to fear from telling the truth, anyway? That was why he was there, after all. "In my brother's sketchbook back at the cottage."

"I would have thought you'd take it straight to the police." Weston turned around fully to face Jamie. "That's why you're here, isn't it? You think I'm somehow involved in his disappearance because of that drawing."

"The police know about it, don't worry. In fact, they're on their way over to question you about it." That might be stretching the truth, but Jamie hoped that all those missed calls and texts meant someone was on their way over here. Felix must have read his message.

"Are they now?" Weston stood up straight; a smile slowly appeared as his whole demeanour changed.

It was so unsettling that Jamie took a step back, almost tripping over the edge of the rug. "Yep."

Somehow, Weston believed he'd got the upper hand, and Jamie had no idea how that had happened. He was the one with the evidence, he should be the one calling the shots, but Weston's confidence had returned in spades and he moved closer until he stood directly in front of Jamie.

Jamie had the sudden urge to turn around and run for the exit, but Weston hadn't told him anything yet. Jamie felt it deep in his bones—Weston knew exactly what had happened to Michael. He held his ground despite the way his hands started to shake.

God, I wish I'd brought Felix with me. His reason for not calling Felix seemed stupid and petty now. Jamie tried for bravado when he spoke. "They'll be here anytime now."

It had the opposite effect to what Jamie intended. Instead of looking worried, Weston grinned at him. "He drew that picture out here, you know. Right where I'm standing now." He sighed as if suddenly lost in thought. "One pencil held tight between his teeth, another skimming over the pages as he drew me. It was... hot."

What? Jamie clenched and unclenched his fists. That wasn't what he'd expected Weston to say, and it must have showed. Weston let his gaze wander down the length of Jamie's body and back up. He licked his lips, and Jamie suddenly felt in need of a hot shower. Felix hadn't mentioned *that* about Weston.

"You look a lot like him, you know." Weston cocked his head to one side as though considering something. "Except for the hair and the fact your attitude is a lot more cynical than his was. He gave me that drawing, said it was a gift for letting him use my balcony to paint on. I didn't realise he'd drawn another one."

Jamie's mouth went dry. Just how many times had Michael been up here? Fucking hell. "He was good at that... drawing things from memory."

"Evidently."

Jamie swallowed down the lump in his throat, not wanting to ask, but desperately needing to at the same time. "So, what happened? The Saturday he disappeared. I know you know wh—"

Weston stopped him with a wave of his hand. "Friday. It happened Friday night, not Saturday."

"But he sent me a—"

"Text message, yes, I know. I watched him type it."

Jamie felt sick. He had a horrible idea where this was going and why Weston was telling him. He slipped his hand in his pocket and found his phone. Thank God for fingerprint access. Sliding his thumb up and across to where the green phone icon should be, he pressed down and then again on the screen, and hoped for the best. He had no idea if he'd managed to call anyone, but it was the only thing he could think of to do.

"I should go." He took a couple of steps back, hit the hard edge of a glass coffee table, and stumbled. "I've taken up enough of your time."

Weston moved so quickly he grabbed Jamie's arm before he could take another step. "Don't you want to know what happened?" His fingers tightened painfully around Jamie's bicep. "Your brother wasn't interested in my less-than-subtle advances at first. Don't you want to hear how I plied him with beer so he'd let me kiss him?" He got right in Jamie's face. "He liked it too."

"You're lying," Jamie hissed. "Michael wasn't gay, and even if he was, he'd never have gone for such a wanker as you."

Weston leaned in so close Jamie could smell a trace of whisky on his breath, and whispered, "He liked it when I shoved my hand in his shorts to jerk him off. Wasn't so keen when I wanted to fuck him, and I do hate a cocktease." He pulled back to meet Jamie's gaze and grinned. "I might have been a bit heavy-handed."

All reason flew out the window as a red haze filled Jamie's vision. "Fuck you, you bastard!" All he could see were images of his little brother struggling to fight Weston off as he beat him. He wanted to kill that fucker for ever laying a hand on Michael.

He shoved Weston backwards as hard as he could, going down with him as he fell to the floor and scrambling on top of him. Not thinking about anything but wiping the smug grin off Weston's face, Jamie punched him again and again, and the satisfying *crack* as his nose broke was like music to his ears. He didn't stop hitting him, and it was only when he found himself pinned under a bloody and battered Weston that Jamie realised that he hadn't bothered to defend himself despite all his apparent strength and Army training.

Weston leaned over him. Blood dripped down his chin and onto Jamie's face. Weston's nose was a mess, his lip was cut, as was his left eye, and he had a handprint around his throat from where Jamie had gripped him. He looked awful, but he smiled down at Jamie with a look of triumph. "So fucking easy."

He pressed down hard on Jamie's hands where he held them trapped above his head, and Jamie winced. "What?" Jamie grit out, his mind still reeling from Weston's earlier words. "I don't und—"

"I lied." Weston spat blood across the table and the rug next to them. "I didn't try it on with your brother—cock's not really my thing."

"So, you just killed him instead?" Jamie spat back, struggling to get out of his grip.

Weston shook his head.

"You fucking did, I kn—"

Weston let go of him long enough to backhand him across the mouth, and Jamie hissed in pain.

"I didn't kill your brother. Unfortunately for him, he overheard something he wasn't supposed to. I dealt with it, but it was too risky to get rid of him straight away. But I am going to kill him. Right after I kill you."

Jamie froze, everything else forgotten as Weston's words sank in. Michael was alive. *Jesus Christ.* "Where the fuck is he? Where's Michael?"

Weston glanced towards the stairs, then back again. "Nowhere you nee—" He stopped and listened for a second.

Jamie heard it too—the faint sound of a police siren, getting louder by the second. *Oh thank God.* He licked his lips, the taste of blood strong in his mouth, but he smiled because Weston was so fucked. "Too late."

To Jamie's surprise Weston laughed. "Perfect timing, actually." Quick as a flash he hauled Jamie up to his feet, wrapped his arms around his neck, and dragged him out through the patio doors.

"What are you doing?"

Weston laughed. "You came here to confront me about the drawing." He started to squeeze his arm on Jamie's windpipe. "I tried to explain I'd never met Michael, that he must have seen me from the top of the path, but you wouldn't listen." Jamie tried to fight back, pulling at the arm around his throat, but Weston only squeezed tighter. "You attacked me. I defended myself, and in the ensuing struggle you fell over the balcony onto the patio slabs below."

"No!" Jamie kicked out at anything he could reach. His foot connected with something solid and a loud *crash* sounded behind them.

"Fuck," Weston hissed and slammed Jamie's head against the door frame.

Jamie saw stars and his head swam. Blackness crept in at the edge of his vision, filling his sight until he lost his fight to stay conscious.

Chapter Sixteen

"Why are you stopping?" Felix turned to glare incredulously at Brierley as he pulled over onto the grass verge. They'd just turned down the side road that lead to Weston's house, as Brierley's phone rang. A huge fucking tractor on the road had already cost them precious minutes and Felix was ready to get out and run. "Just put it on speaker."

Brierley gave Felix a look that said, "I don't bloody think so," and answered the call. He frowned. "Hell—*oh shit!*" He glanced at Felix, shoved the phone at him, snapped "Put it on speaker," and started the siren blaring. They lurched so violently off the verge and onto the road that Felix almost dropped the phone. He quickly put it on speaker as Brierley reached for his radio.

The voices coming from the phone were quieter than normal, as if accidentally dialled from someone's pock—*Fuck,* that was exactly what had happened.

"I should go. I've taken up enough of your time."

"Don't you want to know what happened? Your brother wasn't interested in my less-than-subtle advances at first. Don't you want to hear how I plied him with beer so he'd let me kiss him?"

Oh no. Felix's stomach dropped as he recognised the voices: *Jamie and Weston*. They sped down the narrow lane towards the house as Weston's voice got louder, spilling all his secrets. Felix didn't care if they were getting evidence on him now, because there was only one reason he would tell Jamie all of this, and the next words out of Weston mouth confirmed it.

"But I am going to kill him, right after I kill you."

Brierley swore under his breath, and radioed for backup.

Felix gripped the phone tight, refusing to accept this was the last time he would hear Jamie's voice. "Jesus Christ. Drive faster!"

"Trying."

Weston's house came into view and they broke hard, spitting up gravel and coming to a screeching halt next to Jamie's Civic.

Felix had the car door open before Brierley could turn the engine off.

"I told you to stay inside the car!" The driver's door opened and slammed as Brierley hurried out. "You're not supposed to even be here."

Felix stopped halfway to the front door. He was so used to being in the thick of things, it was hard to stand back and let others take charge, but Detective Brierley was the authority here and Felix needed to let him do his job. Still—

A crash sounded inside the house and Felix met Brierley's gaze for a split second. "Shit. No way am I staying in the bloody car."

They raced for the door. Of course it was locked and didn't budge an inch when Felix kicked it. The thing felt as though it was made of lead.

Fucking hell! Anything could be happening in there.

Felix gave up on the front door and raced around the side of the house, ignoring Brierley yelling at to him.

"Get back here or I'll bloody arrest you!" Brierley was still banging on the door shouting

"Police! Open up!" as Felix skidded to a halt on the patio slabs at the back of the house.

As well as the wrap-around balcony, Weston had a large slabbed area on the ground floor complete with a barbecue and an outdoor dining set. But more importantly it had patio doors leading onto it and one of the doors stood wide open. Felix raced through it and up the stairs to the first floor. He couldn't hear any more banging and prayed that meant Brierley had followed him to the back of the house. He skidded around the corner into the living area in time to see Weston dragging an unconscious Jamie out through the large French doors onto the balcony.

"Westie!" Felix yelled as he raced through the living area to get to them. "Don't fucking move."

Weston paused to look up, his gaze meeting Felix's. He must have known it was all over — Felix had seen him. Whatever he'd planned to do with Jamie was pointless now there were witnesses. He had to know that?

Felix watched with a sick feeling in the pit of his stomach as Weston glanced down at Jamie lying limp in his arms, then back up. Felix saw the exact moment when Weston realised he was fucked… but didn't give a shit.

He smiled back at Felix. "Yet another one you couldn't save, hey, Felix?" Stumbling with the dead weight in his arms, Weston dragged Jamie towards the balcony railing.

Felix ran after him. "No!" He jumped over the low sofa, slipping on the rug in front of it and almost losing his balance, but managed to right himself at the last minute.

Jamie had woken up enough to struggle in Weston's grip, albeit in vain, but it gave Felix enough time to reach them as Weston leaned Jamie against the railing. He bent to grab Jamie's legs as Felix barrelled into him, sending all three of them flying into the glass panels.

Jamie groaned in obvious pain, drawing Felix's attention for a second too long. Weston caught him off guard. He kicked Felix square in the chest, winding him. Felix rolled onto his side to catch his breath. Out of the corner of his eye, he saw the next kick coming and managed to get his hands up, grab Weston's ankle, and twist.

Weston grunted as he fell back onto the decking. Felix crawled over him, landing a couple of punches as Weston tried to sit up, and sent him sprawling back again. He would have carried on; all the hate and anger he'd harboured since Jason's death returned with a vengeance now that he had an outlet, but the sound of handcuffs snapping on stopped him.

He looked up, his arm still raised, to see Detective Brierley glaring down at him as he read Weston his rights. When Brierley finished he called for an ambulance and then climbed over Felix to check on Jamie. "I should arrest you too," he muttered. "I told you to wait in the fucking car."

Felix ignored him, too busy staring at Jamie, who seemed to have slipped unconscious again. He had a split lip and a nasty-looking cut on his temple, with a lump forming underneath it. Felix shuffled over next to him and felt for a pulse in his wrist.

"You can see his chest moving, Felix. He's not dead."

"I know…. I just." He needed to feel it for himself. He met Brierley's gaze, clearly displaying his emotions because the detective clapped him on the shoulder and turned to watch Weston until reinforcements arrived to take him away.

God, if they'd been any later, Jamie would be lying broken on the ground. Weston would have killed him, Felix was sure of that, and the thought of losing someone else he cared about made him sick to his stomach. He let go of Jamie's wrist and held his hand instead, running his thumb gently over the cuts and bruises on his knuckles, and closed his eyes.

Felix watched the ambulance drive away, pissed that he wasn't allowed to go with Jamie. He glanced around, wondering how he was going to get to the hospital, when Detective Brierley came up to stand next to him.

"Come on, I'll give you a lift."

"Don't you have to deal with that?" Felix gestured to where two police officers were bundling Weston into the back of their car.

"Not right away." Brierley pulled his keys out of his pocket. "I want to check in on both Mathews brothers first." He started walking towards his car, and Felix followed him.

Finding Michael Matthews bound and gagged in a hidden cellar wasn't something Felix had seen coming, and he still struggled to believe it. Weston had given him up without much prompting, probably hoping it might help his case when they got him back to the station. Michael was now on his way to hospital too, and Felix hoped there was no lasting damage.

"You should probably get those checked out." Brierley pointed at the cut and bruised knuckles on Felix's right hand.

Now that Brierley mentioned them, they started to throb, and Felix gingerly flexed his fingers. "Later."

Brierley nodded and they drove to the hospital in silence, each lost to their thoughts of what they'd just experienced.

Once through the sliding doors of the entrance, Brierley stopped Felix with a hand on his arm. "I'll be along to take your statement in a while."

"Yeah, okay." Felix gestured at the half-full waiting room. "I'll be right here." He watched Brierley talk to the nurse at the desk before disappearing down the corridor. The plastic chairs looked far from comfortable, but Felix sank down into the nearest one, doing his best to settle. He didn't plan on leaving until he got to see Jamie, and considering he wasn't family, that could be a while yet.

Chapter Seventeen

Jamie came to with a headache. He opened his eyes and immediately shut them again at the too-bright light.

"Oh, just let me—"

Jamie would recognise that voice anywhere.

The scrape of a chair followed and then the room seemed darker, so he tentatively opened his eyes again.

His mum lowered herself carefully into the chair next to the bed and took his hand. "Is that better?" she whispered, then reached up to stroke his cheek.

Jamie nodded and winced. That hurt.

"You have a concussion." She bit her lip, and Jamie met her gaze to see her eyes fill with tears. "Which is lucky for you, because I'd be tempted to hit you myself otherwise. What were you thinking going to that man's house alone? You could have been killed, Jamie!" She might have been talking softly, but her anger and worry came through loud and clear. "You boys have taken years off my life. Years!"

Fragments of memories swirled in his mind. He was too sleep-fuzzy to concentrate on them, but he remembered Weston, the drawing, and… fuck, *Michael*. Then his mum's words finally registered. "Did they find him? Weston said he had him, but—"

She smiled, and this time the tears spilled down her cheeks. "Yes, Jamie. They found him."

"Where is he now? Is he all right?" He tried to sit up, but quickly thought better of it when a wave of nausea swept through him. Ugh, moving was a bad idea.

"Calm down. You'll make yourself ill." His mum leaned forward and put a steadying hand on his chest. "Michael's in a room down the corridor. Your father's with him. He's dehydrated and malnourished, and a lot shaken up, but he's going to be okay."

"Did he say what happened, why Weston kept him there?" Panic gripped him when he thought about his brother being held prisoner all that time. God, Jamie had been to that beach, he'd looked up at the house, and Michael had been there the whole time. He fisted the bedsheets in an effort to stay lying down. What if he hadn't gone to see Weston? Would he have eventually—?

"Jamie, stop." His mum eased one of his hands free from its death grip on the sheets. "We've got him back, so stop worrying. You need to rest so I can take both my boys home." She let out a heavy sigh.

Jamie could only imagine what she and his dad had been through.

The whole thing felt unreal. He'd spent the past two weeks trying to accept that his brother was dead, and now he was lying in a bed down the hall. "Can I go and see him?" Maybe living proof would convince Jamie's mind it was real.

His mum patted his hand. "Soon, sweetheart. They want to keep you in another day for observation, and that means staying in bed and resting. You took a nasty bump to the head."

Jamie reached up, gingerly feeling around the top of his head and his temple. Gauze covered what he assumed to be stitches, because now he was more alert, he felt the pull in his skin. He had a cut on his lip too, and he tongued at it a bit, while he slowly pieced together the events leading up to it. "Yeah. Weston slammed me against the door frame, I think."

His mum muttered something under her breath that sounded like "that fucking cowardly bastard," and he grinned at her.

"Language, Mum."

She shrugged. "What? He is. The police told us what that man was going to do to you, to both of you. And your friend Felix said—"

"Felix? You've seen him?" Jamie met her gaze, and from the small smile on her face, he was being way too obvious about his feelings.

"Jamie." She leaned closer to the bed and her voice dropped to a whisper. "He's been here all night. He hasn't left the hospital since you got in here. Well, only to talk to that nice policeman, but he came straight back as soon as he was finished."

Jamie swallowed past the lump in his throat. "What time is it now?"

She glanced at her watch. "Ten twenty-five."

"Oh." If everything had gone to plan, Jamie would have been on his way back to Nottingham. With no plans to see Felix again—and that had been Felix's choice, not Jamie's. But he'd been waiting at the hospital all this time? It made no sense... unless he felt guilty about what had happened. Jamie turned to look out the window. "Is he out there now?"

"Last time I checked, yes." She sighed. "Want me to go and get him?"

Jamie hesitated. Did he want to see him? His immediate answer was obviously yes, but then he didn't want to find out that Felix was only out there because he thought all this was his fault. Jamie didn't want Felix's attention because Felix felt guilty. "I don't know." He bit his lip, wincing as his teeth caught on the cut.

His mum tsked at him. "Stop that—you're making it worse." She then sighed again and fixed him with her exasperated-parent glare. He felt about fifteen years old again. "Jamie, I don't know what's going on between the two of you, but that boy has sat out there worried sick. If you think he doesn't care about you, then you're an idiot."

Jamie glared at her. "Thanks for that."

She smiled and patted his hand. "You know what I mean. It's obvious he lo—"

"Okay, stop right there." He held his hand up to silence her. No way did he want her to finish that sentence. "I've only known him a week, so let's not get carried away." His mum rolled her eyes but kept quiet, thank God. "And Mum, in case you hadn't noticed, Felix is thirty-two and ex-Army. He's hardly a *boy*."

She laughed at that, a wicked gleam in her eye. "Oh yes, I noticed. I'm not blind. But I'm old enough to be his mum, so he's a boy to me. Anyway, stop changing the subject." She was already half out of her chair, reaching for her stick, when Jamie remembered.

"You should be resting, Mum. What are you even doing making the trip down here?"

She stood up and fixed him with an incredulous look. "I'm taking it easy. You don't see me running up and down the halls, do you? And if you think for one minute I was staying at home after finding out

Michael was alive and you were both in the hospital, then you obviously don't know me very well, Jamie."

"Sorry." He tried not to keep looking at her stick or the way she leaned on it; he'd clearly pissed her off enough.

"So, back to you and that lovely young man out there. Am I fetching him in or not?"

Jamie nodded, his chest suddenly tight with anticipation. "Yeah. Send him in, please."

She stood and leaned over to give him a kiss on his forehead. "I imagine he can answer your questions about yesterday, too."

And he's going to.

Probably not the questions his mum meant, although judging from the knowing look she gave him as she left, he wasn't so sure. He closed his eyes for a second, going through all the things he wanted to ask Felix. Yesterday morning seemed like a lifetime ago, so much had happened. Yet if he tried hard enough, he could still imagine himself in Felix's big bed, with Felix's warm body spooned up behind him. The memory was bittersweet, and Jamie let out a soft sigh.

"Hey."

He looked up, and there Felix was, filling the doorway to Jamie's room as he stood there, looking unsure whether to come inside or not. Felix's clothes were rumpled, his eyes had dark shadows under them, and his stubble was more pronounced where he'd neglected to shave. Jamie hadn't quite believed his mum when she'd said Felix had been waiting. Felix had the appearance of a man who hadn't slept. It made Jamie's stomach clench at the implications.

"Hey," Jamie rasped and turned to reach for the glass of water next to his bed.

"Here." Felix moved quickly to get the plastic beaker for him. "Let me."

He passed the drink to Jamie and stood there looking more awkward than Jamie had ever seen him.

"Thanks." Jamie took a long drink, watching Felix over the rim of the cup. "Mum said you've been here a while."

Felix shrugged. "A few hours."

"More like all night, she said." He gestured at the seat his mother had vacated. It didn't look like she was coming back, and Jamie had had enough of peering up at Felix. "Sit down."

Felix sat and rested his elbows on his knees. It brought him closer, close enough Jamie could reach out and touch him if he wanted. "I had to go and give my statement to the police, but then I… I wanted to make sure you were all right."

"A bit of a headache, but I'll live." Jamie eyed him warily, plenty of questions on the tip of his tongue, but he refused to be the one to do the talking this time. It was Felix's turn, and Jamie wouldn't make it easy for him. He just hoped he wouldn't hate what Felix had to say.

Silence filled the room, the sounds of the hospital filtering in from the corridor outside. Jamie waited patiently while Felix stared down at his hands, clasped loosely together in front of him.

"Fantastic news about your brother," he said eventually, and finally looked up to meet Jamie's gaze.

Although not the topic of conversation Jamie wanted or expected, he couldn't stop the huge smile and the sigh that escaped. "Fuck, I know. Can you believe it?"

Felix shook his head, a small answering smile appearing. "It's a little unreal, but I'm so happy for you that things turned out this way."

Felix seemed genuinely pleased, and Jamie clenched his fists in an effort not to reach out for Felix's hands. It felt like a moment they should be touching in some way, even just holding hands, but Jamie wasn't sure where they stood now. Had anything changed between them? Certainly not for Jamie, but maybe not for Felix either. And he wasn't about to ask again.

Deciding to keep this line of conversation going for now, Jamie said, "Do you know what happened to him? To Michael? My mum didn't say much other than he was a bit of a mess but would be okay. Why did Weston have him there in the first place? What could Michael have done that warranted that? I know you said Weston was bad news, but kidnapping? Imprisonment?" He lay back on the bed, a little winded. The more he thought about it, the more questions he had. "I don't understand." He glanced over at Felix again, hopeful, but Felix sat back in the chair with his arms out wide, palms up.

"I don't know much more than you, I'm sorry. We heard you on the phone, though. Did you do that on purpose?"

Jamie struggled to remember what Felix was talking about.

Seeing Jamie's confusion, Felix explained. "You must have dialled from your pocket or something, because your voices were muffled. But we heard you."

Jamie shook his head. "I don't remember all of it clearly." But thank God he'd had the presence of mind to do that. He could be dead now; Michael would still be locked up. His heart rate ramped up, and he forced those images from his mind. It didn't matter now. They were safe.

"I do know that Weston had Michael locked in what used to be an old wine cellar. Detective Brierley told me. The ground floor of that house was an old cottage before they renovated and extended. Wouldn't surprise me if it was used for smuggling at one time." He looked up and met Jamie's gaze. "I was more concerned with making sure you weren't dead, because *Jesus Christ*, Jamie…." Felix ran a shaky hand across his mouth; guilt was written all over his face. "The drive to Weston's house felt like it took forever. So many images went through my head, and when we got there and I saw him dragging you outside…." Closing his eyes, Felix paused for a moment. Jamie was torn between wanting to drag him up onto the bed to comfort him and wanting him to leave already because it was obvious he blamed himself.

Jamie wasn't a child. He took full responsibility for his own actions. But talking about the fight at Weston's house had started to jog some memories, and this time he did reach out and grab Felix's hand. "I remember other stuff."

Felix frowned. "Remember what?"

Jamie waved a hand impatiently. "Weston was mouthing off at the house. I think a lot of it was bollocks as he goaded me into attacking him, but he said something about Michael hearing something he shouldn't."

"Yeah, we heard that part. I'm sure the police will be in to take your statement soon." Felix gestured down the hall with his thumb. "They're in with your brother at the minute. I imagine you'll be next now that you're awake and alert."

God, Jamie hated being stuck in that bloody bed while everyone got to see his brother but him. As soon as a nurse came in, he was going to insist on going down there. He sighed. "Look, I should have said this as soon as you walked through the door. Thank you for coming to the house and saving my life."

"It wasn't just me, and it was my fault you were—"

"No." Jamie glared at him. "I want to clear something up before the police get here. None of what happened was your fault. I saw the drawing, and it was my decision to go and confront Weston about it. Which in hindsight was incredibly stupid, and I should have waited for the police to handle it."

Felix smiled and nodded. "Yeah you should've. But if I hadn't—"

"For fuck's sake!" Jamie looked up at the ceiling, not wanting to say this next bit because Felix would probably leave then, but he'd had enough of the guilt already. "It was my choice to go there, not yours. So you don't have to hang around the hospital out of some misplaced sense of guilt. Please listen when I say none of this is your fault, so don't feel obligated to stay and keep an eye on me." There, he'd said it. He waited for Felix to say his goodbyes and leave, but he remained seated, staring at Jamie with a mixture of disbelief and frustration.

"Do you really think I'd spend all night in those uncomfortable-as-fuck plastic chairs just because I felt guilty?"

"Well, I—"

"And for your information, you going to Weston's house was partly my fault since I'd spent the last few days telling you what an utter arsehole he was. And if I hadn't given up on watching him, maybe we'd have found your brother sooner. I should have followed my gut. I knew Weston was up to something at that bloody house, but I let it go and you and your brother almost died. So yes, I feel a lot of responsibility for that. But you should have left it to the police. What the fuck were you thinking?" Felix stood and began pacing the room, not looking at Jamie, who now watched him open-mouthed. "He could have killed you! He nearly fucking did, and I would never have had the chance to…."

Jamie swallowed, trying hard not to get his hopes up, but the way Felix was looking at him made his chest hurt in the best way. "The chance to what?"

Felix walked over to the bed, pulled the chair close, and sat down, taking a hold of Jamie's hand. "To tell you what a dick I'd been." Jamie snorted and Felix's lips twitched. "To tell you that you were right. Life *is* too short to let chances like this slip through our fingers because it might be hard work." He linked their fingers and brought their joined hands to his lips, kissing Jamie's bruised knuckles softly. "I came to tell you all this yesterday, only to find you'd done something incredibly stupid and dangerous. It was the shittiest feeling."

Jamie's mouth was as dry as the desert, and his heart raced as he processed exactly what Felix was telling him. He reached over for his water again. "I'm sorry."

"So you bloody should be." Felix squeezed Jamie's fingers gently and kissed them again. "I'm sorry I made you think that I didn't want you, because I do. I really fucking do."

As nice as it was having Felix kiss his fingers, Jamie needed that mouth somewhere else. He tugged on Felix's hand. "Come here."

Felix complied, but instead of the hot and demanding kiss he'd been hoping for, all Jamie got was a gentle press of Felix's mouth on his before Felix drew back and sat down again. Jamie frowned, making Felix grin at him.

"You're injured."

"My mouth isn't," he replied, not liking the whiny tone to his voice, but feeling justified nonetheless. Felix stared pointedly at his cut lip. "Much," Jamie added, tonguing at it.

"Your mum'll be back any minute."

"And?" Jamie scoffed, thinking about what his mum had said earlier. "She already knows how much you lo—like me." God, he was going to kill her for putting that thought in his head. Felix, thankfully, didn't mention Jamie's slip of the tongue.

And talk of the devil, his mum popped her head around the door two seconds later, beaming at them. Either they were grinning like fools or she'd been eavesdropping, because she looked as though she knew exactly what had been said.

Jamie was pretty sure both of those were true.

She smiled at him, and he was amazed how different she seemed. Gone was the haunted look that she'd carried the last couple of weeks. In fact she looked years younger. "I've spoken to the doctor, and if you feel up to it, he said I can take you down to see Michael."

Jamie's breath caught, and he almost leapt out of the bed, but Felix put a hand on his shoulder. "Yeah, please."

His mum slipped out of the room and reappeared with a nurse pushing a wheelchair. Jamie groaned, but she gave him the raised brows and he kept quiet. With careful manoeuvring, they got Jamie into the chair feeling only slightly sick and without flashing anyone in his gown. His hands shook with anticipation as Felix wheeled him out, and they followed his mum's slow steps along the corridor to Michael's room.

Chapter Eighteen

Felix barely stifled a yawn as he pushed Jamie down the hospital corridor to see his brother. It might be due to his lack of sleep, but the whole scenario felt slightly unreal to Felix. Twenty-four hours ago he was lying in bed, watching Jamie get dressed after Felix had told him he didn't want to see him again. What a stupid fucking thing to have done. It very nearly cost Jamie his life, despite him saying it wasn't Felix's fault.

Felix had started the chain of events by pissing Jamie off enough that he went to Weston's house on his own. Felix would carry the guilt over that for a long time.

The one good thing to come out of yesterday's mess was finding Michael. Felix had been sure Jamie's brother was dead, and he was certain Jamie had started to accept it too, and yet here they were about to go and visit him.

Felix hadn't seen much of Michael at the house. He hadn't lied about that. Jamie *had* been his main concern, and everything else was just background noise.

"It's the next room on the right," Jamie's mum — Helen, as she insisted Felix call her — said, and she put a hand on his arm.

Felix steered the wheelchair in through the door and then stopped. The young man lying in the bed, although looking the worse for wear, bore a striking resemblance to Jamie. He had brown curly hair where Jamie's was blond, but their features were so similar Felix couldn't help but stare.

"Can you push me a little closer?" Jamie asked.

"Yeah, of course." Felix snapped out of his daze and wheeled Jamie to the opposite side of the bed to where his dad sat. Then Felix stepped back and leaned against the wall, feeling out of place in what was certain to be an emotional family reunion.

"Fucking hell, Michael, I thought you were dead." Jamie reached out and gripped his brother's hand. Felix heard the hitch in Jamie's voice, and he glanced down at the floor while they exchanged a tearful greeting. Against all the odds, Jamie had a happy ending to his heartbreaking ordeal, and Felix was happy for him. But a small, selfish part of him couldn't help being jealous when he thought of his lack of a reunion with Jason.

They were all talking at once now. Helen sat in a chair near the end of the bed, one hand resting on Michael's foot as she watched her boys with a watery, fond expression, and Jamie's dad sat next to the top of the bed holding Michael's other hand.

Felix's bitterness had no place in this room; he quietly left to go and wait outside. With his head leant back against the wall and his eyes closed, Felix let the muted sounds of the hospital wash over him. Every now and then, the sound of soft laughter floated out of Michael's room, making Felix smile, and slowly he felt the lingering jealousy and resentment fade away. Thank fuck, because feeling like that wasn't something to be proud of.

Felix wasn't sure how much time passed before he heard Jamie calling his name. He sighed but pushed himself off the wall and went back in the room. Jamie immediately beckoned him over to his side, so Felix walked over to stand beside him.

"Felix" — Jamie gestured to his brother while smiling up at Felix — "this is my brother Michael. The cause of all this trouble." Michael rolled his eyes at Jamie, but then turned to Felix with a smile that matched his brother's. "And Michael, this is Felix Bergstrom."

Jamie didn't say anything else, but from the way Michael's gaze swept over Felix and then glanced back at Jamie, it was obvious he'd said plenty while Felix had been outside.

"Good to finally meet you." Felix held out his hand, ignoring the sudden awkwardness in the room.

"Thanks." Michael's grip was surprisingly firm, considering the state of him and what he'd been through in the past couple of weeks. "You too." Michael's face was a little on the thin side, and the dark purple shadows under his eyes made him look drawn, but his blue eyes sparkled with life. "I've heard a lot about you in the last five minutes."

Felix glanced over at Jamie, eyebrows raised. "Is that so?"

Michael's smile widened. "Yep. In fact, Jamie was just saying—"

"Right!" Jamie narrowed his eyes at his brother, making him laugh. "I just need a quick word with Felix before I give my statement to the police." He nodded over at the door. Detective Brierley stood in the doorway. Jamie peered up at Felix, all teasing gone from his face. "Can you take me outside for a sec?"

"Sure."

Felix pushed Jamie out the door after saying his goodbyes to Michael and Jamie's parents. Brierley greeted him as they passed and told Jamie he would meet him in his room in about ten minutes.

"Might as well take me back there now." Jamie pointed down the corridor.

"Okay."

They were silent on the way back to Jamie's room. Felix had a good idea of what Jamie wanted to talk to him about, and he welcomed it. The events of the last day or so were starting to catch up with him; fatigue was settling into his muscles and making his head fuzzy. He needed to sleep, but only after they sorted things out between them.

With the door shut and Jamie back in his bed, Felix slumped down into the chair and sighed.

Jamie reached out for his hand, and Felix took it. "You look knackered."

"Thanks." Felix yawned immediately afterwards and laughed. "I feel it."

"I'll make this quick, and then you can go home and get some sleep." Jamie squeezed his hand to get Felix to meet his gaze. "I'm going back to Nottingham as soon as Michael's discharged, which they're hoping will be tomorrow or the day after."

"Oh." In all the excitement, Felix had forgotten about Jamie leaving. "So soon?" The words were out before he could stop them. Of course, Jamie would want to be at home with his family after everything that had happened. "That'll be good for all of you." He smiled and tried not to let his disappointment show.

"Yeah, it will. But I meant what I said before. I want to keep seeing you." His smile faltered when Felix didn't say anything. "I thought you said—"

"I did." Felix sat up straighter and leaned forward. "I do... want to keep seeing you too, I mean. I was waiting to hear how we're going to do that."

"Oh." Jamie snorted. "Like I have all the answers."

Felix relaxed at Jamie's teasing tone and the easy way they slipped back into the relationship they had at the cottage. "Well, you seemed to have it all figured out yesterday morning."

"I was bluffing. All I knew was that I wasn't ready for this to end." Jamie glanced down at their joined hands. "I hadn't thought much beyond that."

They sat staring at each other until Felix yawned again. "Christ, sorry." He rubbed his eyes with his free hand.

"We don't have to decide anything now. I'm not going anywhere for a day or so at least, and even then it's only a few hours up the motorway." Jamie tugged on Felix's hand until he got the message and leaned over his bed for a kiss. "It's enough that I know you want this," he whispered as Felix pulled back to meet his gaze.

"Yeah?"

Jamie nodded. "Yeah. So go home, get some rest, and then come and see me later. I'll have worked out all the logistics by then."

Felix stood and eyed him dubiously. "Really?"

"Probably not, but come back anyway."

Felix kissed him again, then reluctantly stepped back, letting go of Jamie's hand. "I'll see you in a few hours, then." He lingered in front of the door, not wanting to go, but dead on his feet.

"For God's sake, go home before you keel over. I'll be right here waiting for you to get back." Jamie's smile lit up his whole face, crinkling his eyes at the edges.

Felix's insides warmed. It was the best thing he'd seen, and now, since he'd got his head out of his arse, he'd get to keep seeing it. Even if that meant weekends only for a while, they'd work something out. And that was enough for now.

Epilogue

Four months later

Jamie grabbed his holdall, slung it over his shoulder, and picked up his car keys from the mantelpiece. In the hall, he paused at the bottom of the stairs and shouted up, "Michael? I'm off now. See you Monday."

Five seconds later, Michael's shaggy-haired face appeared at the top of the stairs.

"You need a haircut." Jamie frowned. "You're starting to look like a tramp."

"Fuck off, the girls love it."

Michael grinned down at Jamie, the sight making Jamie's heart stutter for a second as he remembered how close he'd come to losing him. It happened less and less as the weeks passed, but Jamie thought it would never go away entirely. He smiled back. "They're lying to you."

"Yeah, whatever." Michael jogged down the stairs and wrapped Jamie in a tight hug. "Love you. Have a great weekend." It was a thing they did now, his mum and dad too. No one brought it up — it happened by unspoken agreement. Because you never knew what was around the corner. Jamie had said that so often lately that Felix had threatened to tattoo it on his *bloody forehead*. But it was true.

"Thanks. You too." Jamie followed him to the front door, but Michael turned to face him before opening it.

"Did you and Felix talk about Weston?"

Jamie set his bag down and leaned against the wall. "Yeah."

Karl Weston had sung like a bird once in police custody, offering up any information he had to get out of serving time in jail. Turned out he'd had nothing to do with Jason's death, but he knew who was responsible, and that was what Michael had overheard him talking about that Friday night. Weston, fearing for his life if anyone found out he'd let it slip, had kept Michael prisoner while he figured out what to do with him, and he'd staged Michael's things on the beach. The threat of prison obviously trumped Weston's fear of retribution, though, and in exchange for providing the police with several names in conjunction with Jason's death, Weston had got off relatively lightly. In Jamie's opinion, anyway.

"And?" Michael prompted.

"I think Felix is just glad to have someone being held accountable."

Michael nodded. "Yeah, I guess that makes sense." He reached down and picked up Jamie's bag, holding it out to him. "Are you going to tell him your news tonight?"

Jamie sighed. "No. I'm going to bring it up, and then we'll discuss it like adults. That's what you do in a relationship."

Michael scoffed and pointed at the boxes in the living room, already half-packed with Jamie's things. "Really?"

Maybe Jamie had got a bit ahead of himself, but he was so tired of only seeing Felix at the weekends. Sometimes they couldn't even make that, and Jamie went two weeks or more without getting to touch or kiss him. And he missed him.

Christmas had been so good, with both of them having over a week off work, but it made the inevitable separation that much harder. Jamie was done.

He shrugged, ignoring the smug look on his brother's face. "I'm being optimistic, that's all."

"Like he's going to say no. You might as well take it all down with you now and get it over with. He's going to be ecstatic."

Jamie couldn't stop the wide smile, nor did he want to. "I hope so."

Michael reached around him and opened the door, shoving Jamie none too gently through it. "Go before your disgusting happiness makes me ill. I've got plans."

"Okay, okay." Jamie turned as he got to his car. "Take care, yeah?"

Michael nodded, serious this time. "You too."

With a final wave, Jamie got in his car and set off on the two-and-a-half-hour trip to see Felix.

Jamie had set off early enough to miss the worst of the traffic around Reading, but Fridays were generally shit once you got past lunchtime. He arrived at Felix's house just after four, pleasantly surprised to see Felix's car already parked outside.

He let himself in with the key Felix had given him over two months ago and set his bag down in the hall. "Hey."

A crash and a muffled curse sounded from the kitchen. Felix appeared, looking hot and sweaty, with traces of flour on his cheek. "You're early."

Jamie walked over to him, admiring the way Felix's T-shirt clung to his shoulders and biceps. Felix worked out regularly and went running—Jamie didn't know where he found the time, but he appreciated the results. "Yeah. I missed you. Two weeks is way too long." He slid his arms around Felix's waist and kissed him, holding him close and relaxing into his warmth.

Felix hummed against his lips, opening up and slipping his tongue into Jamie's mouth. He tasted of coffee and cinnamon. Jamie chased the familiar flavours, moaning and pressing closer. The Starbucks near Felix's office building had spoiled him for ordinary coffee, and Jamie had bought Felix a coffee machine for Christmas so he could make his own when Starbucks stopped doing the Christmas specials.

"I missed you too." Felix kissed the side of Jamie's mouth, then nipped along his jaw down to his throat, while Jamie closed his eyes and enjoyed Felix's touch after twelve long days apart. Felix had worked through the last weekend to get a project finished, but now he had Monday and Tuesday off.

Jamie intended to make the most of their long weekend, reacquainting himself with every bit of Felix several times over. But first they had things to discuss. Hopefully that wouldn't affect the second part of his plan. "Why are you covered in flour?"

Felix backed him up against the wall in the hallway and pinned him there with his hips pressed tight to Jamie's, and Jamie gripped Felix's arms.

Damp cotton covered Felix's shoulders and back as Jamie ran his hands over him, prompting him to add, "And why are you all sweaty?"

Felix stopped kissing a hot trail along Jamie's collarbone and looked up. "I was cooking dinner." He stared at Jamie for a few seconds longer, his gaze intent and heated, making Jamie's toes curl, and then he went back to kissing the base of his throat. "Wanted to surprise you."

Jamie reached down for the bottom of Felix's T-shirt and tugged it up until Felix raised his arms so that Jamie could take it off him. "While that sounds like a lovely idea, I think dinner can wait."

"Yeah." Felix pulled at Jamie's belt buckle, undid it, and then popped the button free on his jeans. "Takeaway sounds better, anyway."

"Mm-hmm." Jamie was halfway through taking off his T-shirt when Felix dropped to his knees and undid Jamie's zip. "Oh fuck."

"Later."

Jamie felt Felix's grin against his belly, and he melted into the wall, laughing. "Whatever you say."

But Felix already had his mouth full.

Twelve days was far too long to go without this—without Felix's hands and mouth on him. Too long to go without waking up with Felix's big warm body wrapped around him. Jamie bit his lip, losing himself in the slick glide of his cock in and out of Felix's mouth, and vowed to never go that long without seeing him again if he could help it.

"I have something important to ask you," Jamie blurted, his brain-to-mouth filter clearly offline. Now was not the time for this conversation.

Felix pulled off with a huff of laughter and stared up at him. "Seriously? Can't it wait?"

Jamie nodded. "Yes, absolutely. Ignore me. My brain is fried from your awesome blowjob skills."

With a smile and a shake of his head, Felix licked the head of Jamie's dick and ever so slowly sucked him back into the slick heat of his mouth.

"So good." Jamie sighed and settled back into it, determined to keep his mouth shut this time.

But then Felix pulled off again and sat back on his heels. "Is it something I should be worried about?"

It took a couple of seconds for Jamie to focus on what he was saying. "What? Why have you stopped?"

"Because now I need to know what you wanted to ask."

"It can wait. Really." He took Felix's chin in his hands. "Please. I've missed you touching me."

Felix stood, which was the opposite of what Jamie wanted, until Felix grabbed his hand and tugged him towards the stairs. "Then let me do it properly."

Once inside the door to Felix's bedroom, they shed their clothes, laughing as they tried to kiss and walk at the same time and failed spectacularly. Jamie collapsed onto the bed and pulled Felix on top of him, kissing him breathless.

"Turn over," Felix whispered, kneeling up and reaching for his bedside drawer.

Jamie complied and moaned in pleasure as Felix trailed kisses down his back and worked slick fingers inside him, teasing him into a writhing, panting mess.

"Come on." Jamie glanced back over his shoulder, meeting Felix's gaze. "Please."

Felix nodded. Moments later, Jamie's focus narrowed to the feel of Felix pushing into him, and then taking him apart with slow, powerful thrusts.

They fucked as though they had all the time in the world, hands clasped together and pressed into the mattress on either side of Jamie's head. Soft sounds filled the room—moans and muttered curses—until Felix took them over the edge and Jamie cried out, spilling onto the quilt underneath him.

"Shit." Jamie huffed out a laugh as Felix lay on top of him, letting him take all his weight. "I hope you haven't just changed the sheets."

Felix sighed against the side of Jamie's neck, his warm breath making him shiver. "Worth it." With another heavy sigh, Felix carefully pulled out and rolled onto his side, facing Jamie. "Now what was so important you felt it necessary to interrupt a perfectly good blowjob?"

Jamie smiled. His post-sex glow chased away any doubts he had that this suggestion wouldn't be well received. The way Felix looked back at him made his heart swell, and Jamie reached out to cup his jaw. "I can't keep doing this. I thought I could but weekends aren't enough."

Felix tensed. "But—" He swallowed and covered Jamie's hand with his own, his expression stricken. "What are you saying, exactly?"

God, that was not the look Jamie wanted to put on Felix's face. *Stupid, sex-addled brain*. He shuffled forward and kissed him softly, then rested their foreheads together. "I'm saying that I love you, and I don't want to spend another day wishing I was with you instead of miles apart." Felix's breath hitched and Jamie smiled. "I'm saying that if you want, I'd like to move here and live with you. I realise that I've just invited myself to move in with you instead of waiting for you to ask, but I—"

Felix put his hand on Jamie's lips. "I love you too." He smiled. "But I have something to tell you." He moved his hand when Jamie tugged on his fingers.

"Oh?" Jamie would have been nervous but for the way Felix was smiling at him.

"I don't want to be without you either, but I won't make you move away from your brother when you're only just getting over nearly losing him."

Jamie shook his head. He hadn't made the decision lightly. Leaving Michael and his mum and dad would be hard, but he had to live his own life, and that meant having Felix in it full-time. His family understood and were more than happy for him. "No, I—"

"Jamie, listen. You don't have to move down here, because I'll be coming up to you."

"What?"

"A contract came up in Nottingham. I already interviewed for it."

Jamie stared at him open-mouthed, barely able to contain his excitement. "And?"

Felix leaned in and kissed him. "I start four weeks on Monday. Already handed my notice in."

The only reasonable response to that was for Jamie to pull him back in for another kiss, but he was smiling too wide for it to last long. "You always have to have the last word."

Felix shrugged. "I take it you're happy with that?"

"Fuck, yes." Jamie had been prepared to move, would have happily done so, but having Felix *and* his family was better than anything. "And if you give me half an hour, I'll show you exactly how happy I am."

Felix laughed and rolled them over, pinning him to the bed. "That a promise?"

"Yeah." Jamie looked up at him, seeing everything he felt reflected back at him. His heart stuttered. "We might be here for a while."

With a sly smile and a slow roll of his hips, Felix leaned down to whisper in Jamie's ear. "Sounds about perfect to me."

Jamie wrapped his arms around him and held him tight, still reeling from the fact he was getting everything he wanted. "Yeah," he said, closing his eyes. "It really does."

About the Author

Annabelle Jacobs lives in the South West of England with her three rowdy children, and two cats.

An avid reader of fantasy herself for many years, Annabelle now spends her days writing her own stories. They're usually either fantasy or paranormal fiction, because she loves building worlds filled with magical creatures, and creating stories full of action and adventure. Her characters may have a tough time of it—fighting enemies and adversity—but they always find love in the end.

www.annabellejacobs.com
Twitter: @Ajacobs_fiction
Facebook: Annabelle Jacobs Fiction

Email: ajacobsfiction@gmail.com

Also by Annabelle Jacobs

The Choosing

Torsere Series:
Capture
Union
Alliance

The Lycanaeris Series:
The Altered
The Altered 2
The Altered 3

Toy With Me

Will & Patrick Series:
A Casual Thing
A Serious Thing

Magic & Mistletoe

Share Your Experience

Thank you for reading *Chasing Shadows.* Reviews help other readers find books. Please consider leaving a review for this story on the site where you purchased it, or on Goodreads.

Made in the USA
Charleston, SC
18 March 2016